THE DREADFUL OBJECTS

CHRIS COOPER

The Dreadful Objects

Published by Dreadful Media

ISBN: 978-1-7323949-0-2

Enjoy the book? Please consider leaving a review at goodreads.com or amazon.com. Every review helps.

To receive news of new publications, events, and exclusive offers, please sign up for the Dreadful Media Newsletter on our website.

WWW.DREADFULMEDIA.COM

For Mom, Dad, and Sterling

SPECIAL THANKS

Jacob Mathers
Jill Collet
Maggie S
Olivia Lewis
Pam and Darryl
Petra Gisela Sørensen
William Wesley Morton

CHAPTER ONE

JAMIE HUNG HIS ARM OUT of the car window and straightened his fingers to form a wing. The feeling of the wind guiding his hand up and down reminded him of car rides he'd taken as a kid, a feeling he would never tire of. Lilly sat in the driver's seat next to him. Her hair was up in a ponytail, and the sun caught her red highlights. They drove up and over the hill leading to the bridge into town. He couldn't remember where they were going, but he knew it was important.

The car crossed over the expansion joints and onto the bridge. Surprisingly little traffic was on the bridge this time of day. The sun flashed on his face as the steel beams crossed its path.

"What does it feel like to die?" Lilly asked.

"What?" Jamie thought he'd misheard.

"What does it feel like to die?" She asked the question as if asking for the time, with no emotion except for innocent curiosity.

He looked over at her, and she was staring back at him, eyes wide and empty.

"Jesus, Lilly, watch the road!" he said, startled by her vacant gaze.

She grinned widely but kept her eyes locked on him.

His heart rate increased, and he turned his head just in time to see an oncoming car. After a flash of white light, everything went black.

He came to, lying in darkness, his eyes half shut. The bedroom furniture was familiar, but something wasn't right. A group of black figures hovered over him, shifting in and out of focus. One of them held up a shiny metal object.

Something was binding him to the bed. He tried to move his arms, even to simply blink his eyes, but he was frozen in place. The dark form brought the metal object closer to his chest, and he could just make out the sharp edge of a scalpel.

They think I'm dead. They're going to cut me open.

Panic set in as he tried to think of a way to show he was still alive, that he hadn't perished in the crash. A dull groan grew from his chest and up through his throat until it became a full-blown scream.

Sweat flung from his forehead as he bolted upright in bed. The figures had vanished. His dog Buttons was caught off guard by the sudden outburst and fell off the end of the bed. As Jamie recovered from the nightmare, he needed a few moments to realize the ringing of his phone had pulled him from sleep.

He looked at the phone screen and tapped the button to answer the call.

"I'm so sorry. It must have happened again. I owe you a beer, man," he said, out of breath.

Deshawn lived in the apartment below him and was fortunately a pretty friendly guy. "Just making sure that you're all right. I'm going to hold you to that beer, though."

Jamie hung up the phone. He thought he'd finally gotten over the sleep paralysis, but this episode brought the feeling of terror rushing back. The first time it had happened, one of his neighbors must have thought he was being murdered and called the police. Usually, it occurred when he was stressed or had indulged in a few too many drinks, but he hadn't had anything to drink in a while and had done his best to numb his emotions in other ways. The time was only four in the morning, but sleep rarely came after one of these traumatic episodes.

Jamie slunk out of bed and headed toward the kitchen for a glass of water, with Buttons close behind him. The tiles were ice-cold against his skin, and he quickly tiptoed over to his house shoes, next to the small island. He pulled a pitcher of filtered water from the fridge, poured a glass, and chugged. Buttons whimpered and sniffed nervously at the door, a clear sign that he sorely needed to go out.

I must have scared the piss right out of him.

He threw on a pair of shorts, sitting on the kitchen stool, and grabbed Buttons' leash from the junk drawer. He loved his pup, but taking him downstairs to pee in the middle of the night was a pain in the ass. As soon as the door opened, Buttons dashed for the stairs. His favorite tree sat in the field across the street from the apartment complex.

A chill was in the air, and Jamie wished he had something on besides shorts and a wife beater. As soon as Buttons had done his business, Jamie dragged him back across the street and into the complex. The dog loved to be outside, regardless of the time of day, but the night was too cold to indulge him any longer. Jamie dreamt of a house outside the city, where Buttons would have a backyard to run around and explore freely. Given the student loans and his low salary, the house in the country wasn't happening anytime soon. For now, Buttons would have to settle for the tree in the lot across the street.

Jamie started a pot of coffee, moved a stack of ungraded papers from atop his laptop, and sat down to check email. After a moment, his eyes adjusted to the bright light from the screen. The video clip he'd been watching the previous day was still on the screen. It was from one of those reality-show music competitions and featured an unattractive father of four, who shook nervously on stage. The judges gave their obligatory eye rolls as the man mentioned he'd be singing "The Prayer." Their cynicism turned to awe as he belted out the notes in perfect pitch. Jamie was ashamed to admit it, but he sometimes spent an hour or more watching clips like this to lift his spirits. *If only a hand would descend from the sky, pluck me out of this life, and place me in another.* He hoped someone would discover something valuable in him, sitting just below the surface. For the time being, he'd have to settle for another person's glory and the small hit of dopamine that came with it.

His inbox was devoid of anything interesting and cluttered with coupons and newsletters. Out of desperation for entertainment, he opened his junk folder and scanned for anything remotely interesting. Amidst a sea of Nigerian princes and male-enhancement spam, he noticed a message from someone named Donald Ash from Ash and Associates. Surely this was some sort of phishing scheme, attempting to separate him from the dollar or two left in his bank account, but he clicked anyway.

Jamie,

I'm sorry to inform you that your uncle, Thomas Joseph, has passed away. We are in the process of settling his estate, and you are listed as the primary beneficiary. Unfortunately, it appears that the number that we have for you has been disconnected, so I apologize for having to send the unfortunate news via email.

You can reach my office at the number below. Please feel free to give my secretary a call at your convenience to schedule an appointment to go over Mr. Lawson's estate.

I am very sorry for your loss.

Sincerely,
Donald Ash

Jamie sat back in the chair. He hadn't heard from his uncle in more than a decade, so the sudden reference surprised him. The proper spelling and personal references made the message seem just authentic enough for him to do a bit of web research. He opened a new browser tab and typed the name of the firm into the search engine. There were several results for Ash and Associates, but he navigated to the page of the one located in Cincinnati, where his uncle lived. Sure enough, the number on the contact page matched the number from the email. The message was legitimate.

"My uncle's dead," he said aloud.

He hoped to feel a twinge of sadness but instead felt nothing. He had seen so much death in his life over the past two years that it had lost its emotional impact. This disconnection sometimes made him feel separated from his body and thoughts, as if he were watching life happen to him on a television screen. The fact that he hadn't seen his uncle for many years compounded his emotional chilliness. The guy was a recluse and didn't even bother to come to his own brother's funeral when Jamie's father passed away.

Against his better judgment, he decided to give Ash and Associates a call once their office was open. He set a reminder on his phone and lay down on the couch. The warm glow of the TV washed over him as he mindlessly flipped through the channels.

CHAPTER TWO

"**G**O TO BED," JAMIE SAID, pointing at the crate.

Buttons had no interest in the crate. In fact, he loathed the crate.

"Go to bed," he said again, more forcefully.

Buttons lowered his head and walked into the crate. He gave a low grunt as he plopped down into his doggie bed and looked longingly up at his owner.

"I'll be back tonight buddy," he said. "I'd take you with me, but I don't want to leave you in the car all day. Deshawn will take you for a walk later."

Jamie heard the cries from the other room as he grabbed his coat and left the apartment. The drive to Cincinnati from Pittsburgh was nearly five hours long, so he'd have plenty of time to fantasize about what awaited him. The term "estate" brought to mind a posh house, Ferraris, and piles of gold. It was certainly a departure from the whitewashed apartment and the middle-class tragedy that had become his life.

Ash and Associates sat in a yellow-brick building in the middle of an old town square. The name of the company was emblazoned in big gold letters on the front window, which made it hard to miss. Jamie's tires hummed against the brick road, and he found a place to park on the street, along the side of the building. He walked around to the front entrance and pulled open the heavy oak doors. The interior was dimly lit, and the walls were covered with fleur-de-lis wallpaper and dark wooden molding. A receptionist was barely visible behind the massive reception desk, and her beehive hairdo appeared to be older than the antique desk itself.

"Help you?" she wheezed, exerting the smallest amount of energy possible. Her voice was deeper than Jamie's and must have resulted from years of frequent smoke breaks.

"I'm here to see Don Ash regarding T.J. Lawson's estate. I have an appointment."

Saying "Don Ash" as two separate words was hard, but the secretary understood. She waved him through the side door and into the main office area. Ash and Associates seemed frozen in time, filled with leather wingback chairs and grand desks. The carpet was forest green and reminded him of the old carpet in his elementary school. He did a double take at an old rotary phone sitting on one of the desks.

"Jamie?" someone said from behind him.

He turned around and smiled in affirmation.

"It's nice to finally meet you. I'm Don, the manager of Mr. Lawson's estate," the man said with an outstretched hand. He was short and stout with curly hair and a widening bald spot at the top of his head. His mustache lent an absurd touch to his already cartoonish look.

"Nice to meet you too," Jamie replied.

"Please, come into my office and have a seat," he said, guiding Jamie through the doorway of a nearby office. "We've got quite a bit to discuss."

Don gestured for him to take a seat and walked over to an antique drink cart. He uncorked a large decanter and poured an amber liquid into a glass tumbler.

"Brandy?" he asked.

His watch read one in the afternoon, but Jamie had no place else to be.

"Please," he replied.

Don poured a second glass and sat down across from him. He slid one of the glasses across the desk.

"You know," he said. "It took me years to develop a taste for this stuff. I had a client that would send a bottle to the office every year for Christmas. I used to give it to one of the interns. When the client passed a few years ago, his widow came to the office to sign some paperwork. She noticed a bottle that I'd left on my desk and told me that her husband had purchased the very last cases of it at an auction years ago. It was made in the city where he'd proposed to her. She didn't drink much, but she'd share a glass with him on special occasions. When he was diagnosed with cancer for the first time, he gave up drinking completely, so he'd give the bottles away to his closest acquaintances. I don't know what I did for the guy to make the list, but ever since I heard that story, I've had a fondness for it. Of course, I reserve it for special occasions."

"And what makes this a special occasion?" Jamie asked.

"Your uncle was a close friend of mine. I handled most of his financials, and I'm pretty sure that I was the only one to whom he spoke regularly. He wasn't exactly right in the head, but he was a good guy. You probably haven't read the story, since it only made the local papers in Cincinnati, but your uncle killed himself a week ago. I'm sorry to be meeting with you under these circumstances, but you are listed as the primary beneficiary in his will. The man had a considerable estate, and he's left nearly everything to you."

Jamie slid back in his chair, and the leather cushion made an unfortunate squeak. He knew his uncle had been a well-known writer in the mideighties to nineties, but he knew little more of the man than what appeared in the yellowed *New York Times* article his father had kept in a photo album. He hadn't even read his uncle's books. T.J. was a solitary man who never married or had children. Jamie's dad had kept in touch with him every now and then, but he had passed away two years before. Jamie was still affected by the sudden loss of his father, and he felt a tightness in his chest whenever he came to mind.

The thought of being the only little branch left on his grandparents' family tree produced a gnawing pain deep inside Jamie's gut. He was an only child whose mother had died of cancer before his fifth birthday. His father, Paul, fought to pay for his schooling, keep him fed, and make sure he had some semblance of a normal childhood. While no childhood was completely normal, love had given Jamie a fighting chance.

"Doing okay, son?" Don asked.

"Oh, sorry, lost me there for a minute." He snapped back to reality.

Don removed a file folder from a stack on his desk. He flipped through until he found the summary page, which listed T.J.'s primary assets.

"The two biggest items in the estate are a home in the city and, of course, monetary assets. If you look here,"—Don pointed—"you'll see the sum of his liquid holdings."

Jamie read the highlighted line but had a hard time processing what he was seeing. Someone appeared to have forgotten to add a decimal point to the number.

"Three million?" It sounded just as absurd aloud as it looked on the page.

"That's right, a little over three million in liquid assets. There are stocks as well as a few other securities, but your uncle also kept a tidy amount in cold, hard cash," Don replied. "T.J. also has a safety-deposit box, but I'll have to see if I can dig up a key for it first."

Jamie wasn't sure what to make of all of this. He picked up the tumbler from the desk, put it to his lips, and tipped it back, emptying the rest of the brandy into his mouth. The shock of instant wealth was too much. He wasn't sure whether the cause was the brandy or the three million dollars, but his eyes began to water. He took off his glasses and wiped the corners of his eyes with his thumb and index finger.

"Why don't we go to the house and take a look around?" Don asked. "Looks like you could use some fresh air."

CHAPTER THREE

ON WATCHED AS JAMIE'S SUBARU pulled through the wrought iron gate. A playful devil sat atop the archway, keeping close watch on any who dared to enter. Its eyes always seemed to follow Don when he came to visit, which gave him the creeps. The car's wheels spun on the gravel driveway, leaving a cloud of dust in their wake. It came to a halt in the shadow of the imposing Italian villa-style home. Don rolled down the tinted window of his black Lexus and waved at Jamie. He grabbed the elaborate set of keys sitting on the seat next to him and climbed out of the car.

Turner House sat nestled in the back corner of an affluent subdivision on a hill overlooking the houses on either side. It looked largely out of place next to the art deco and Frank Lloyd Wright–inspired homes that speckled the neighborhood. It also predated the other homes by nearly fifty years and sat with the wisdom and presence of a building that had seen significant moments in history.

"It was built by a meatpacking titan in the late 1860s," Don said, walking toward Jamie. "Most of the original features and materials are still intact, but as you'll notice, your uncle took a few liberties with the decorations."

He walked up the front steps and unlocked the tall double French doors then waved Jamie through the entryway. As Jamie walked inside, a life-size model of Boris Karloff's iconic portrayal of the *Frankenstein* monster greeted him, and he nearly tripped backward out of the doorway.

"Sorry, I should have warned you about Franky. I've been here a few times, and I still haven't gotten used to him," Don said.

"Dad told me stories about T.J.," Jamie said. "He said that while he was out seeing his girlfriend or sneaking a beer with his buddies, T.J. would go out by himself. The only things that he'd ever sneak out to see were horror movies."

T.J. had loved monsters, killers, and ghosts of all kinds, and he spent his days dreaming of new and sinister creations, which ran loose in his mind. He published his first book, *Satan's Song*, a few years after his high-school graduation. The story revolved around a demonic music box that ensnared people with its eerie tune. The book would go on to be the first in a planned *Dreadful Objects* trilogy and was followed by *Cellulose*, which featured an old film reel that caused those who watched it to go insane. Despite the simple premises, he developed a cult following, which led to a moderate amount of success for an author with only two published works.

Turner House became the ultimate symbol of the author's success and an outward expression of his inner personality. He was reserved on the outside but housed all sorts of demons within. He lived there for nearly a quarter century and succeeded in filling every corner of the mansion with all the creepy-crawly things that skittered out from the corners of his imagination. The house became his muse, and all the artifacts inside had served as fuel for the nightmares he created for his readers.

Jamie ran his fingers along a row of specimen jars that sat on a shelf next to the entryway.

"What's going to happen to all of this stuff?" he asked.

"That's completely up to you. The house comes with everything inside of it, and you'll also receive what remains of your uncle's financial assets, once his estate is settled. I'd hate to see his collection dismantled, but I would be happy to connect you with an auctioneer. Some of this is probably worth a bundle," Don said.

Don couldn't deny that the house was a feast for the eyes. Every nook and cranny was stuffed with horror props and memorabilia. It was all covered with a thick coating of dust but was still an incredible sight to behold. Still, he'd felt an added sense of dread since discovering its owner's body in the cellar. He tried to temper his feelings in front of Jamie, who was too overwhelmed by the situation to notice anyway. He wanted to hand over the keys to this place as soon as possible and move on with his life. In his mind, Turner House was no longer a home but a mausoleum.

"This is all so unbelievable," Jamie said. "I haven't even seen my uncle in years, and now everything is mine? I just can't process this."

"Life's funny sometimes, isn't it?" Don replied.

"What about his funeral? Will I need to help make the arrangements?"

"Taken care of," Don replied. "T.J. laid everything out in his will, and the arrangements are paid for."

He guided Jamie up the staircase, lined with old movie posters and anatomical drawings in the spirit of Da Vinci's famous sketches.

The pocket doors leading to the office were in need of some repair, but Don managed to slide them out of the way.

"This is where he did most of his writing," he said.

The doorway opened into a large room with a twelve-foot ceiling, and the walls were lined with recessed bookcases, all filled to capacity with books of various shapes and sizes. An old Royal typewriter sat in the middle of an intricately carved mahogany desk, with a piece of paper nestled in its carriage. A few lines appeared to be typed out at the top of the page. Across from the desk sat a wooden display case with three glass domes. One held a music box and another a movie reel, and the third was empty. They must have been props from T.J.'s first two books. *What had he planned for the third one?*

Don plopped down in the desk chair.

"This is pretty much how I found it," he said. "Except he also left a neatly folded pair of pants and sweater next to the typewriter. Never did figure out why exactly. Maybe he wanted to make things easier to clean up."

"Did he give any reason why? A note or something?" Jamie asked.

"There was a handwritten note on the stack of clothing. The police held a short investigation into his death but were quick to confirm that it was suicide. They bagged the note during the investigation, along with the clothing, but I'll never forget what it said." He recited the note to Jamie word for word.

Don,

I've done my best to shut out the demons, but they persist. I'm surrounded by the death and destruction that I've created, and there's nothing that I can do to fix it. I've tried. I'm sorry to leave you like this. Thanks for being a friend. There's no need to come back next week.

P.S. Stay out of the wine cellar.

T.J.

"I typically came by every few weeks to check in and go over T.J.'s most recent royalty and financial statements, but this time, he didn't answer the door. He wasn't exactly outgoing the last few years of his life, but he was certainly punctual. I knew that something wasn't right and let myself in. When no one replied to my calls, I climbed the stairs towards the office and noticed that the door was left ajar."

Don was holding back his emotions in favor of cold irreverence, but he could feel tiny cracks forming in his veneer as he retold the story.

"I wish he would have talked to me, you know? We weren't best friends or anything, but I probably saw him more often than anyone else."

"What happened to him?" Jamie asked.

Don was tired of reliving the events of that day, but he figured this would likely be the last time. He should have heeded the warning in the note, but instead he rushed to the wine cellar. Some part of him thought T.J. was still alive, and he would never have forgiven himself if he didn't try to save his friend. His memories of the grim scene were photographic, embedded in his mind, no matter how hard he tried to forget the details. He descended the stairs to the cellar and turned the corner into the main chamber. An empty bottle of wine lay toppled on the ground, along with a broken wine glass. He traced the floor stones with his eyes until they were obstructed by a shadowy mass on the floor. The gun that T.J. used to kill himself must have blown apart with the first shot. The police would later identify it as an antique pistol from his collection. The poor cellar lighting spared Don from some of the grisly details, but it had been falling directly on T.J.'s face, and his expression still haunted Don.

Jamie's eyes grew wider as the story progressed, and Don noticed a twinge of emotion in the boy's face. It wasn't pity or discomfort. It was empathy.

Don stood, trying to shake off the heaviness of the moment. "Anyway," he said. "It certainly wasn't the best day of my life."

"Thanks for all of your help," Jamie said. "For what it's worth, and it feels weird saying this, but I'm sorry for your loss. It seems like you may have been the closest thing that he had to a friend. I know I'm his nephew, but I hardly knew the guy."

This caught Don completely off guard, and his voice cracked as he spoke. "We worked together for a very long time. The guy was nuts, but there was a lot to like about him." He paused. "Made all of my other clients seem pretty boring."

The two stood in silence for a moment.

"What about that page in the typewriter?" Jamie asked. "What's on it?"

"He must have been working on some sort of writing project. It doesn't have anything to do with all this," he replied.

Jamie walked over to typewriter and twisted its carriage knob to free the piece of paper. They read the lines on the page. It was indeed the final page of a story, but the rest wasn't there. Jamie placed the page on the table, next to the typewriter.

"So, what happens now?" he asked.

"Well, there's still some paperwork involved. Fortunately, I managed all of your uncle's assets, so I won't need a lot of time to round everything up. Just need to make sure to cross all of the t's."

Don led Jamie out and headed back to his car. As he turned the key in the ignition, he gave the mansion one final look through the windshield. He couldn't help but feel that the house was watching him while he pulled away as if it were alive. Soon enough, it would be out of his life forever as well as all the tragedy that had come with it. It was Jamie's burden now.

Jamie finished signing all the paperwork back at Ash and Associates by early afternoon. With the last stroke of the pen, he was now the owner of Turner House and the millions that came with it.

CHAPTER FOUR

JAMIE STARED INTO AN EMPTY closet. Once filled with colorful dresses and skirts all smelling of lavender, it now stood as a reminder of love lost. More than a year had passed since his partner, Lilly, had passed away. At first, he preserved everything just as it had been before she left for her mom's that day. He left her wardrobe in the closet, her books on the shelf, and her glasses on the bedside table. Nearly everything in the apartment reminded him of Lilly, and one night it all became too much to bear. In a fit of anguish-driven rage, he bagged up all her belongings in several black garbage bags and chucked them into a dumpster. Now, the only physical things that remained from their relationship were the apartment and the dog, the only thing that brought a splash of color to Jamie's life. He was eager to rid himself of the apartment, but his pup was a constant companion in a world full of abrupt change and loss. Buttons was part Australian cattle dog and part mutt, and his favorite hobby was spinning around until dizzy.

Lilly had named him for the speckles of caramel in his white coat.

Stacks of cardboard boxes towered in the corners of the apartment. The walls were bare now, leaving the off-white paint the only color in the room. He stretched the packaging tape over a box of books and decided to break for lunch. Although he loved to read, it was a joy only recently discovered. He had taken nearly ten years to undo the hatred for reading that high school had instilled in him. That in itself was comical since he was now a university professor. It was often said that teachers are the worst students, but sometimes the worst students become the best teachers—at least, he liked to think so.

Jamie resigned from his educator position at the local college in Pittsburgh shortly after signing the inheritance paperwork. Along with the house and everything inside, he received nearly two million dollars after the estate had been settled completely. That also came with the rights to T.J.'s two previous works and a monthly royalty check. Most would be relieved if they were told they would never have to work again, but no amount of money could completely wash away the discontent tingeing his reality. Still, it offered some reprieve.

Buttons watched the movers from the apartment window. He barked and paced as he tried to warn Jamie of the evil thieves stealing all their stuff. The coarse hair on his back was standing on end like a mohawk. That always happened when he became scared or protective, and Jamie couldn't help but laugh.

The apartment felt cavernous now, and his voice echoed from wall to wall. He stared at the empty spaces where he and Lilly had binged on TV shows, argued about movies, and eaten dinner. Even though the physical things were gone now, every corner and every surface still held some memory of her. He looked at the stove where he had once set a towel on fire while trying to surprise Lilly with a pork loin and brandy sauce. Instead of being angry, she draped caution tape across the stove to tease him. Even though most of his memories in this place were happy ones, the apartment was a constant reminder that he'd never be able to make new ones with her.

Jamie sat at the kitchen table to thumb through his hiring packet for the university in Cincinnati. He'd originally moved to Pittsburgh for the teaching position, but now he had no reason to stay. The town was isolating without Lilly, plus a mansion was waiting for him in Cincinnati. He knew he needed some time to sort things out but also knew he'd go stir crazy without some sort of job. He had accepted an adjunct position and would teach a few courses at the university. It offered extreme flexibility and would allow him to reconnect with a close friend from school. Sarah had been Jamie's high-school classmate, who taught history at the arts-and-sciences college in Cincinnati. In fact, she was the one who sent the call for an adjunct to him.

He looked forward to rekindling a friendship or two that predated his life in Pittsburgh.

"Time. I just need a little time and some new scenery," he told Buttons, patting him on the head.

The moving men finished loading the truck and left for Cincinnati. In five hours or so, plus the pit stops for the dog, he would be in his new home, starting a new life. Jamie stood in the doorway of the apartment one last time. Pretty soon, someone else would move in and make their own memories there. The place was just a shell now, and soon no evidence would remain that he'd ever lived there. He jiggled the dog's leash, which sent Buttons into a frenzy, and the two headed for the car.

The Subaru was loaded with the most fragile of Jamie's possessions and, of course, Buttons, who had proven to be pretty durable, considering his weekly tumbles down the stairs. The apartment complex grew distant in the rearview mirror as the car pulled away. Five hours in the car seemed like an eternity to Jamie, but Buttons could never spend enough time hanging his head out a window.

Jamie stopped short of the turnpike to grab some snacks and a coffee. He pulled into Ed's Truck Stop Deluxe and parked next to the grassy lot beside the store. After Buttons did his business, Jamie put him back in the car. The dog watched with a pitiful look on his face as Jamie locked the door and headed inside. Although Buttons had been left alone thousands of times before, he always looked as if he wasn't positive that Jamie would return.

The aisles of the truck stop were filled with cigarette-lighter-powered coffee pots and panini presses. Jamie marveled at all the trucker contraptions and gadgets and briefly considered leaving everything behind for a life on the open road. Then he passed a wide array of hemorrhoid cream and quickly reconsidered the alternative career choice.

He grabbed a pack of turkey jerky and some sunflower seeds from one of the snack-food aisles and walked over to the coffee pots. The wall of coffee was overwhelming. *Since when did gas stations carry twenty varieties of coffee?* He settled on a coffee, or what he assumed was coffee, called Electric Reaper. Apparently, it would either provide enough of a boost to power him through the next few hours of driving, or it would kill him.

On the walk to the cash register, Jamie noticed a wall of CDs and audiobooks. *The Shining* and *The Hobbit* both sat on the bottom shelf. As he crouched down to pull them from the lineup, he lost his balance. He managed to save his cup of Electric Reaper but fell into the shelves and sent a dozen or so plastic jewel cases crashing to the floor.

"Doing all right over there?" asked a pimple-faced clerk, who popped his head out from one of the snack aisles.

"I'm fine, thanks. I just get really excited about audiobooks," he replied, trying to joke away his embarrassment.

"Don't we all?" said the clerk sarcastically and made his way around the aisle to help.

The two collected the fallen soldiers and started filing them back into their proper rank on the shelf. Jamie took the opportunity to browse the titles that scattered on the floor. The clerk picked up a few cases, and Jamie noticed he was holding a copy of *Satan's Song*.

"I'll take that one if you don't mind. Might as well buy something since I caused such a mess," he said, gesturing to the case in the clerk's hand. The clerk handed it over and finished sorting the titles on the floor.

Jamie cradled the CD set under his arm and took the rest of his loot to the cash register. Buttons bounced around the back seat in excitement as he saw Jamie exit the store and head back to the car. After fighting with the plastic packaging, he freed the CD from the case and slid it into his stereo.

Night fell on the old Victorian home as Annabelle explored every crack and crevice that the house had to offer. Although her family had only lived there for a few days, she covered each of the house's three floors extensively. All that remained was the basement. She hummed to herself as she descended the staircase, the old wooden steps creaking beneath her feet. The walls were covered with chipped mortar, which exposed the seeping stone wall underneath it. Annabelle gazed into the endless darkness of the far corner of the basement. The light bulb was busted, but she had come prepared with a flashlight.

It took her a few moments to realize that she wasn't alone. She stopped humming, but something continued to carry the tune. The sound surrounded her as if it were coming from the walls. Although she was terrified, there was nowhere to run because the sound was everywhere. The walls appeared to swell and recede as if they were breathing. A few loose bricks fell to the ground and shattered, causing Annabelle to leap backward. She noticed a small opening where the stone had fallen away and held her flashlight up to it. Something shiny caught the light. Annabelle reached inside and pulled out a small music box.

Buttons gnawed on a piece of jerky while Jamie took a sip from his coffee cup. He was starting to understand why his uncle's books were so popular. He too loved stories of monsters, ghosts, and demons, but something about this story felt different. The characters weren't simply cardboard cutouts who served as demon fodder; T.J.'s characters had hopes, dreams, and personality. He could feel their fear as if they were real.

CHAPTER FIVE

"**S**ARAH!" JAMIE WAVED TO GET her attention. Sarah wore a brightly colored sundress with a pair of flip flops. Her brunette hair was shorter than it had been in high school. She also had significantly less acne and had ditched the braces. He found it hard to let go of his mental image of the nerdy girl who'd always had her face buried in a book.

"Jamie! Good to see you. How have you been?" she asked.   He stood to greet her, and she came in for an awkward hug.

"Not bad. It's been a busy few days, but things are going pretty well," he replied.

"Good! I'm going to grab a drink. What did you get?"

"Just a regular coffee."

He had shamefully tossed away the two breakfast-sandwich wrappers before Sarah arrived. The trip to Turner House had taken much longer than expected due to some unexpected traffic, and he was too tired to go out to dinner.

Jamie's eyes followed her to the counter. He was glad to see a familiar face completely detached from the events of the past two years. While most had stopped asking him how he was feeling and if they could do anything to help, they still looked upon him as if he were someone to pity. He hated being pitied.

"So, when did you get into town?" Sarah's question pulled him out of his thoughts.

"Yesterday, actually. I've been here long enough to sleep a bit but haven't touched any boxes yet," he replied.

He had tried to sleep in T.J.'s bed, but the lumpy mattress and odd sense of bedroom decor made it nearly impossible. A life-size figure of a yeti stood menacingly in the corner of the bedroom, and a large group of crows was suspended from the ceiling, with another particularly evil-looking bird perched atop the bedpost. He recalled that a group of crows was referred to as a "murder" but tried to rid that word from his mind for the night. He told her none of this, of course. Jamie wasn't sure if she knew anything about his uncle T.J., but he didn't want her to associate feelings of being creeped out with his presence.

"Wow, you must be exhausted. We could have done this some other time," she said, sipping some sort of foamy concoction.

"Oh no, no, it's perfect. I needed some time with a familiar face and a coffee. Did you know that gas stations sell extra-caffeinated coffees now? The jolt is great, but the crash is wicked."

"I had no idea," she laughed.

Sarah's looks might have changed, but her laugh was the same as it had ever been.

"The house is going to take a bit of getting used to. I knew that my uncle was an odd guy, but you should see this place," he said.

"I've read about it, actually. Your uncle's collection was featured in the paper a few years ago. Haven't you read about him?" she asked.

"Not really. I knew that he was well-known, but I hadn't read any of his books until just yesterday. *Satan's Song*. I just started. Have you read it?" he asked.

"I've read both of them, actually," Sarah replied.

"Of course you have," he said.

She used to let him copy off her book reports in high school since her love for reading complemented his hatred for it.

"Have you decided what to do with all the stuff? I'm surprised that you aren't being hounded by collectors," she said.

"Well, T.J.'s lawyer is fielding any calls for me now. I haven't decided what I'm going to do with all of it. I've been thinking about selling it, but it was the guy's life, you know? He must have spent decades building the collection. He even has the music box and film reel on display in his office."

Sarah's eyes lit up. "You have to show me sometime," she said, visibly excited by the prospect of a tour. "You know, he was a local celebrity of sorts. He became a recluse after publishing his second book, and rumor had it that he went insane."

"I think that's been firmly established."

They sat at the table for an hour or so, recalling stories of school dances and teenage angst. Although much had changed since high school, Jamie still saw glimpses of the girl he'd spent so much time with in his formative years. As they talked, the distance between what was and what had been seemed to shrink. They were different people now, but the same traits that had brought them together were still there.

CHAPTER SIX

Annabelle's arm shook as she tried to keep hold of the antique lantern. Her fingers ached as a powerful force seemed to lift them away, one by one. She fought to keep control of her hand, to shut out the voice that told her to let go, but the force was simply too powerful. The lantern seemed to spit fire as oil and flame spread across the carpet.

By the time the first firetruck had arrived, the house was already engulfed. The firefighters tried to save the family inside, but the weakened structure crumbled around them and made it too dangerous to continue the search. Everyone and everything in the house was completely destroyed, all except for a wooden music box pulled from the smoldering rubble.

Jamie stopped mopping for a moment to take in the ending of the book. He could see the image of the little girl in his head, setting her home ablaze. That was a dark twist, but he understood that the forces of good don't always triumph. He'd learned that lesson on the middle-school playground. The final passage seemed oddly familiar to him. He thought back to the typed page T.J. had left in the typewriter. Although he couldn't remember the passage exactly, the characters were the same.

The page still sat next to the typewriter, untouched since he'd moved in. Jamie sat in the office chair and read the lines on the paper.

```
Annabelle stood on the edge of good
and evil as a powerful force tugged
her toward the darkness. She felt
herself losing control of her hand,
which threatened to drop the oil
lamp on the living-room carpet.
As her hand trembled, she thought
of her parents, sleeping in their
bedroom on the second floor. She
fought to keep control of her arm,
and just as she started to let go,
her mother clenched Annabelle's
hand tightly, preventing the lamp
from falling to the floor.
```

That's weird. Why would T.J. rewrite an ending to a story that was already published? Jamie thought the published ending was a bit of a downer, but it was certainly a better ending than what he'd found in the typewriter.

Jamie took a solid week to clean the house and remove the layers of dust from the countless artifacts his uncle had on display throughout it. He could have paid someone to do it, but his classes didn't start until the next day, and he had plenty of time to kill. Idleness tended to take him to a dark place, so he tried his best to stay busy. Many of the shelves were full of medical and animal specimen jars, which looked as if they hadn't been cleaned in years. He found a display of anatomical models particularly hard to clean since each organ had to be removed and dusted one by one. Not only did the cleanup keep him busy, but it also gave him a chance to get to know his uncle, even if posthumously.

A minuscule stack of cardboard boxes sat in the corner of the dining room. They seemed tiny when compared to the massive mansion and all the knickknacks living inside. After a thorough cleaning of the house, Jamie slowly unpacked his belongings. A small plastic zip-top bag sat at the bottom of one of the boxes. In the last desperate throes of packing, Jamie had simply started dumping the contents of his drawers and cabinets into boxes, and the bag must have been buried in one of his desk drawers.

He slid the contents of the bag out into his hands and sorted through the pile. Instead of souvenirs and photographs, Jamie hoarded tickets. Aside from old movie stubs, he found lift tickets from when he and Lilly would go skiing and an admission ticket covered in Japanese symbols. Work had sent him to Tokyo a few years before, and Lilly was able to take the week off and go with him. They stayed in a tiny hotel room barely larger than the bed itself and visited the Edo Museum in their free time to explore the history of Japan. He was more adventurous then and even talked Lilly into trying boiled octopus and fermented squid. He hadn't done anything spontaneous in a long time, and the memory of the trip seemed far away.

Jamie left almost all his uncle's things in place for the time being, except for T.J.'s unique wardrobe, which he swapped out for his own. Looking at the remnants of his uncle's life, he still felt like a visitor in someone else's home.

While Jamie removed a decade's worth of grime from nearly everything in the house, Buttons busied himself exploring the recesses of Turner House's massive back yard. The yard and gardens sat in stark contrast to the inside of the house. T.J. kept a small groundskeeping crew on the payroll, so everything was neatly trimmed and maintained. Buttons disappeared among the flower beds, but every once in a while, Jamie would see his head pop up from behind a hedgerow. This was heaven compared to the dog's typical pit stop.

Jamie took a lunch break and ate a sandwich as he flipped through a copy of the newspaper at the kitchen island. He thought back to the newspaper article his father had showed him as a child. That little clipping contained more information about T.J.'s life than he had ever gleaned from the man himself. And now, he sat in the middle of T.J.'s mansion, eating a peanut-butter-and-jelly sandwich. Jamie thought of how sitting alone in this giant house for a decade or two must have felt. He could sympathize with T.J. because of his own lonely nights in the apartment after Lilly's death, staring at a computer screen at four in the morning or lying on the couch all day, watching TV. He didn't pity the man—he feared becoming him.

Jamie reached for his phone and pulled up his conversation with Sarah. He typed out a new message: *Just finished cleaning the house. Still interested in a tour?*

She replied a few minutes later. *Absolutely! When were you thinking?*

He tapped out a response. *What about tonight? Have plans? If not, come over, and I'll cook.*

I have a faculty meeting until 6 but could be there around 7. That work?

Perfect!

CHAPTER SEVEN

J AMIE WAS STRAINING A POT of boiling pasta when the sound of the buzzer caused him to jump, dropping the pot into the sink. Buttons sat patiently, watching the cooking adventure unravel and hoping for the inevitable burnt remains. Jamie wasn't accustomed to cooking with a gas stove, and the house's large six-burner antique had proven quite the adversary. His pan-seared pork chops quickly devolved into blackened hockey pucks, and he received several burns, not realizing how quickly direct flame heats metal. He recovered quickly by tossing the chops, saving one for the dog of course, and putting a pot of water on to boil. Pasta puttanesca it would be. He strained the noodles then dumped them back into the pan.

The source of the buzzing wasn't clear at first. He had no idea where the call box was located, so he stood in the entryway and waited for Sarah to buzz again. The sound came from a small speaker box, hidden behind a dead potted plant. Jamie pushed the pot aside and pressed the intercom button.

"House of Horrors. Who's there?" he asked, hoping Sarah was indeed at the gate.

"Just a dim-witted damsel who comes bearing wine," she replied.

"Say no more. The gate's open. Just push. I'm in the kitchen."

Buttons appeared to be too preoccupied by the sights and smells in the kitchen to greet the guest at the door.

Jamie heard a yelp from the entryway. He had completely forgotten the life-size Frankenstein that greeted Sarah at the door.

"Sorry about that! He doesn't bite," he shouted from the kitchen.

Sarah came around the corner, red-faced but smiling. "Any other lifelike nightmare machines that I should know about?"

"I'll have to show you the yeti in my bedroom," he replied before realizing that sounded slightly dirty. "There are a few other ones here and there, but it wouldn't be any fun if I told you. You'll discover them on the tour," he said, recovering.

"Fair enough. If there are many more surprises like the one at the door, I'm going to need a glass of wine first."

"The corkscrew is in the drawer over there." Jamie pointed at a drawer two steps over from where she was standing. "Took me nearly an hour to sort through all of these drawers to find what I needed to cook. I figured that we might need a corkscrew."

"This kitchen is incredible. I can't wait to see the rest of the house," she said, removing two glasses from the wine rack above the bar. "Want a glass too? It's pinot noir."

"Um, sure. I'm pretty ignorant when it comes to wine. Pinot noir is red wine, right?"

"Yeah, it's pretty mild compared to some of the other reds. I should have asked what we were having for dinner. I could have brought a different one."

"Well, the pork chops kind of fell through, so I've moved on to pasta," he replied.

"Oh, perfect! It should go well with it," she said, pouring the glasses a little fuller than usual. The setting sun cast a brilliant orange glow over the kitchen.

Jamie was proud of his puttanesca. It probably wouldn't make the top-ten list of meals cooked in the Turner House kitchen over the last hundred years, but it trounced the grab 'n' go meals he'd been living on. He was also drinking the wine faster than he should but noticed Sarah was keeping up.

"It's so nice of you to invite me over for dinner," she said.

"It's my pleasure. Plus, Buttons and my uncle's lawyer have been my only real company over the past few days."

"Well, at least you have the yeti to lull you to sleep, plus I'm sure you'll be hearing from Clara if you haven't already."

"Clara... Who's Clara?" Jamie thought he'd misheard Sarah.

"Well, if you inherited the house and everything inside, I'd say that she's your ghost."

"Ha! My ghost? I didn't know that this house was supposed to be haunted." He was amused, but his staunch skepticism of anything paranormal precluded fear.

"You mean you didn't know about Clara? She was one of the Turner girls. You've heard of Joseph Turner, right? The man who built this house?" she asked.

"My uncle's lawyer mentioned something about the house being built by a bigwig in the meatpacking industry, but he didn't really go into any details," he replied.

"Joseph Turner was one of the key players in the Cincinnati pork industry. Pork was so big here that they actually nicknamed the city Porkopolis in the 1800s. Eventually, Chicago pulled ahead in the industry, and Turner was one of the leaders in the battle to keep Cincinnati on top. He helped to fund a giant stockyard in the city in an effort to increase capacity and beat Chicago." Jamie could feel his eyes glazing over, and Sarah must have noticed, for she stopped the story short.

He was just happy that pork was off the menu for the night.

"Sorry, I'm a history nut, so I geek out about this sort of stuff. I'll spare the details, but Turner built this house and lived here with his five children. He was pretty successful for a long time but put a lot of money into the stockyard, most of which he never recovered. As the industry left the city, his empire started to crumble. Then, one day, his daughter disappeared while playing in the backyard. Despite all his remaining money and influence, he couldn't find her. The police abandoned the search after a few months of looking."

"That's terrible." Jamie's eyes widened.

"It's not as terrible as the rumors that followed. Apparently, some of the house staff came forward to the police regarding Turner and his fits of rage. On more than one occasion, staff saw Turner beating his children, and apparently he locked them in broom closets for hours if they misbehaved."

"You mean broom closets like the one over there?" Jamie pointed at the door on the other side of the room, and Sarah turned to look with wide eyes.

"Let's go check it out. Maybe Clara wants to say hello." He felt he was being slightly mean but couldn't help himself.

"No, I think I'll pass. You go ahead, though." She grinned.

He rose slowly, with a painfully serious look on his face. He noticed the dog, sleeping on the floor with his squeak toy beside a barstool. As he walked away, he nudged the squeak toy with his foot. Buttons started to rustle as Jamie walked toward the door. As he opened the door, the dog bit into the toy, which let out an aggressive squeak. The timing couldn't have been better, and Sarah squealed, jumped up from her stool, and spun around.

"Thanks for the assist, bud," he said. "This is just the wine cellar. Should we pick out another bottle just in case? There are probably tons down here, but I may need your help."

Most of the light switches in the house were old push-button switches, and Jamie traced the wall with his fingers, looking for the one that would light the basement. A dim yellow bulb flickered on above the staircase, and he beckoned Sarah to join him.

"I guess we can start the official tour here," he said.

They carefully descended the old staircase and turned the corner into the cavernous wine cellar. Rows and rows of different wines sat there, some covered in dust that appeared to be decades old. The cellar ran the length of the house, which was impressive but not as impressive as the mural adorning the walkway. Sarah walked along the corridor, staring at the endless shelves of wine.

"Look down," he said.

She lowered her head and stared down into a vast hellscape. The stone floor was painted to look like glass that allowed the onlooker to see the depths of hell below. Flames shot upward, and damned souls were poked and prodded by little demons. The scene progressed as she walked along the hallway, eventually leading to the throne of the Dark Prince himself.

"Is this standard for wine cellars nowadays?" she asked.

"Only in wine cellars owned by crazy horror authors."

"Well, it doesn't look like we have many choices. Anything stick out to you?" she asked sarcastically.

"More of the same would be fine for me," he replied.

Jamie decided to spare Sarah the story of his uncle's suicide until they were safely back in the kitchen. Don had told him the cellar had been cleaned up of any nasty reminders of that day's tragic events, but Jamie went down earlier just to be sure. The mural had a few splotchy areas that he assumed were caused by the chemicals used to clean the bloodstains.

"It looks like your uncle favored the reds too. There are a few over here that look pretty new." Sarah swiped her finger down one of the bottles and held it up for him to see that it was free of dust.

"This one looks pretty nice. Have you heard of Domaine de la Romanée-Conti before?" Jamie stumbled over the name on the label, partly because it was a name he'd never seen before and partly because he was starting to feel the fuzzy effects of the wine.

Sarah walked over where he was standing. As she reached for the bottle on the shelf, her hand grazed Jamie's. "Oh, sorry," she said, pulling her hand away. "Sure, you want to go for that one? It might be worth more than everything I own combined."

"Well, I'd say that we *have* to open it, then."

They turned back toward the staircase and returned to the kitchen. Buttons was waiting at the top of the stairs, whining nervously.

"So that's where he killed himself, then?" she asked casually.

"Wait, how did you know? I was going to tell you but wanted to wait until we were upstairs," he replied.

"Read it in the paper," she said.

Jamie had forgotten his uncle's local celebrity status. *Of course the story had made the paper.*

Sarah gave him a lesson on why a wine needs to breathe. She wasn't concerned about the cheap bottle she'd brought, but this one deserved to be treated with respect. She searched the cabinets for an aerator and decanter and poured the remainder of the pinot noir as Jamie watched intently.

"This is supposed to accelerate the breathing process," she said. "You might not be able to taste the difference with the wine that I bought, but you'll be able to tell with the other. We may not get to that bottle tonight, but you have to promise me that you'll use the aerator if you open it on your own."

"I promise," he replied.

She took the decanter and wine glasses into the dining room.

The table was pristine, with two perfect place settings. Jamie'd had to look up table-setting tutorials online, but he was pretty proud of how everything looked. He'd decided that a candle might be too forward, so he bought some freshly cut flowers from the grocery store and placed them in a vase that he found under the sink.

He plated the pasta, and they both sat down at the dining-room table. Sarah looked around the room and took in all the obscure objects surrounding her. A curio cabinet of old medical devices sat in one corner, and the walls were lined with framed antique maps. Jamie wondered if she was more excited for the tour than she was for dinner, but he didn't blame her if that was the case.

"Everything looks great!" she said.

"Thanks. Aren't the dishes incredible? The silverware's real silver too. Thought it would be fun to pull all this stuff out. It looked like T.J. hadn't used any of it for years."

"How was the place when you found it? I imagine it must have been a wreck," she said, forking her pasta.

"The kitchen was a nightmare, but it seemed like he didn't use much of the house. Everything was dusty, but only a few areas appeared to be lived in."

Dinner went well, considering its abysmal start with the pork chops. Sarah filled Jamie in on everything he would need to know about his upcoming position. She worked in a different department but knew some of the key players in his. The politics were familiar to him, but the fact that he was a lowly adjunct meant that all he had to do was show up and teach. He could ignore the rest of the traditional baggage that usually came along with teaching at a university, but he still enjoyed Sarah's dramatization of it. She gestured wildly as she told stories of the injustices she had encountered on campus. The room felt alive with her in it, and he realized how much he'd missed real conversation. Apparently, she felt the same way.

Sarah was three years into her faculty position at the university and had just submitted all her documentation for reappointment. She said the last six months had been pure hell, leaving her little time for cooking, socializing, or other generally healthy habits. With reappointment behind her, she was determined to take some time for herself.

After dinner, Jamie put all the dishes in the sink and started the grand tour. They ascended the main staircase, but Sarah only made it halfway up before having to stop and gawk.

"What's wrong?" he asked.

"Do you know what this painting is?"

He hadn't paid much attention to the picture before. It was a painting of a girl who had enormous eyes, in a blue dress.

"Uh, a creepy girl with big eyes?" he asked.

"It's a Margaret Keane. This was her thing, girls with large eyes. This is incredible! It's probably worth a fortune!" she said, gawking at the painting.

"I had no idea," he said, trying to add an extra dose of surprise to his voice to make up for the fact that, to him, the painting was a little off-putting. "If you think this is cool, let me take you to my uncle's library."

Jamie opened the doors at the top of the stairs, and Sarah walked across the threshold as if she was Alice walking through the looking glass. She was immediately drawn to the glass cases that protected T.J.'s real-life Dreadful Objects.

"No way!" She rushed over to the display cases. "Can I open them?"

"I don't have a problem with it, but they're locked, and I have no clue where my uncle left the key," he replied. He'd made that discovery while dusting that morning.

"Well, they're supposed to be cursed anyway, so it's probably for the best," she said with a disappointed smile. "You know, his final book was supposed to be about this house," she said. "I saw an old interview clip online, and he mentioned that he moved here for inspiration. Apparently, he was fascinated by the Turner family and the possibility that something sinister happened here."

The Turner story was new to Jamie. He knew the house was old, but he hadn't read anything about it. If Clara was indeed haunting Turner House, she now had T.J. for company.

"So, what happened to him?" she asked. "The paper said that he killed himself in the cellar, but it didn't give many details. He lived here for decades, didn't he? But he never published his final book."

Jamie told her the story of the suicide note and the death in the cellar. He still didn't understand what T.J. had meant when he said he was surrounded by death but figured that was just the result of the mind of a depressed fiction writer who spent too much time alone.

Sarah absorbed every detail of the story. She stepped over to the writing desk and sat in the chair. She was especially creeped out by the fact that T.J. had removed all his clothes and folded them neatly in his office before making his way down to the cellar.

She sat for a few moments, taking in the story and looking at the display cases across the room. In her excitement, she had completely overlooked the Royal Standard No. 1 typewriter that sat on the desk.

"What a gorgeous typewriter, and this desk is unbelievable," she said, forgetting her momentary horror.

"I guess a great writer ought to have great tools," he replied.

"I can't believe that this is what he used to write his books, or at least I assume that he used it to type them?"

"I don't think that T.J. was a big computer guy, so that's a good bet," Jamie said.

"Do you have any paper?" she asked. "Can we try it?"

"There's probably some paper in one of the drawers. Let's see." He knelt down and tugged at the first door—locked. The second revealed typing ribbon and a few pencils. The third was a success, and he pulled a few pieces of blank paper from the stack.

"Here you go," he said as he handed the paper to Sarah.

She rolled the paper into the typewriter carriage and curled a finger around her lips, contemplating what to write. She leaned over to type.

```
Sarah was very thankful for the
evening's meal and company. It was
getting late, and she had to work
the next day, so she knew that
she better be on her way. Jamie
understood but was sad to see her
go. They walked down the stairs
together, and Sarah invited Jamie
over for dinner and a movie next
week. He, of course, accepted.
```

"Well, who am I to argue with a bulletproof plan?" Jamie said.

"Great! I'll give you a call, and we'll figure out when we want to do it."

She stood up to leave the room. He looked at the typed page and chuckled. She was certainly no Hemingway, but the lines lifted his spirits. He wasn't sure if Sarah knew how much the night had meant to him, but he didn't care. It was the most fun he'd had in quite some time.

They walked down the stairs together and stood at the doorway for several minutes, saying their goodbyes. Sarah turned to leave but then turned back to Jamie.

"It's so great to see you again," she said and wrapped her arms around him. "It's good to have you back."

Jamie stood at the doorway and watched her walk down the gravel drive to her car.

CHAPTER EIGHT

SCREAMS ECHOED THROUGH THE CORRIDOR. Jamie ran as fast as he could to the door at the end of the hallway and pressed his ear against it to verify the source of the sound. He reached down to turn the doorknob but found nothing where the doorknob should have been.

"Use the keypad, you dolt." Buttons was sitting in a nearby rocking chair, reading a newspaper and smoking a pipe. He stared judgmentally as Jamie looked for the keypad. The door was padlocked, and no keypad was in sight.

"Here, let me do it. I'll let you in from the other side." The dog grunted as he fell onto all fours and went through the doggie door. "Never mind. There's no room for you in here," he said from the other side of the door.

Jamie grew frustrated and took a running leap, shoulder first, at the door, which fell flat on impact. He tumbled forward onto his stomach. As he stood up, he was shocked by what he saw. The room was cylindrical, and the stone walls were covered with dozens, if not hundreds, of portraits. He looked up toward the ceiling, but the walls seemed to stretch indefinitely into the sky as if Jamie was at the bottom of a deep well. The portraits were all of girls with irregularly large eyes, all of which were trained on him.

The screaming started again, with increased intensity.

"I'm in the painting!" someone screeched, begging for help.

"Which one?" Jamie asked the room. They all looked the same to him.

"The one by the yeti," the person replied.

He turned and saw the yeti, who seemed to be juggling bottles of wine in the distance.

"In here!"

Then he noticed the source of the sound. Sarah was standing on the other side of the painting's frame, her eyes larger than any of the other girls'. She was wearing a blue-and-white checkered dress.

"Thank God you found me!" she yelled, gesturing for him to come closer.

"Come on, let's go!" he said.

"First, kiss me," she demanded.

"What? There's no time for that," he said.

However, she was already planting one on his forehead, then his cheek, then his lips. But something was wrong. Her lips were dry and cracked. He tried to pull away, but she grabbed his arms and held them tightly. He wrenched himself away from her and noticed she had changed. She wasn't Sarah anymore. She was Lilly, but her face was gray and decayed. The skin had receded around her lips, and her eyes were sunken into the back of her head. Jamie spun around and tried to run, but the door was nowhere to be found. The characters in the paintings had all transformed into corpses, rotting and falling to pieces as the walls crumbled around him. He opened his mouth to scream, but no sound emerged.

A warm blanket of fur surrounded him. It turned out to be Buttons, who was sprawled across his chest. Jamie's face was covered in a fresh coat of dog slobber. This wasn't the first time the dog had pulled him out of a nightmare.

"Oh gross!" Jamie pushed Buttons off, but the heaviness of the dream still weighed down on his chest. He wiped his eyes, crusted over with tears. This was the first time in a while that he'd cried in his sleep. Sadness had become his job, and he accepted it as a permanent part of his life, but the last few days had been different, almost joyful. Perhaps this was his body telling him that he didn't deserve the reprieve from grief. *And what was the kiss with Sarah all about?*

He walked to the bathroom for a glass of water then returned to bed. Although the bedroom was terrifying at night, the large windows captured an enormous amount of light during the day. The sun streamed in, filling the room, and he allowed the warm rays to wash over him. Waking up to the sun was certainly better than waking up to dog breath.

Jamie climbed back into bed and checked his phone. *8:16*. His first class was at 11:05 this morning, and he was eager to get back into a routine. He lay there for a few minutes, browsing his news feed, then hopped out of bed. The stairs creaked as he went downstairs to the kitchen. Buttons was close on his heels, but he still hadn't figured out how to navigate the hardwood floors and slipped as he turned the corner toward the staircase. He ran to the food bowl and sat patiently as Jamie scooped a cup of dog food out of the hilariously large bag in the cupboard. He stepped out onto the back porch to take in the morning. The fence surrounding the property *did* offer privacy and protection, but it also somewhat detracted from the beauty of the gardens. Jamie returned to the house and made some eggs with toast, which he ate at the kitchen island.

The drive to work was a short one, a mere five minutes up the hill. He could have walked if he really wanted to, but Jamie wanted to give himself enough time to find the classroom. The campus was alive with activity. Students were navigating to their first classes, and a DJ had set up shop in the middle of the main street, blaring the top forty through a set of large portable speakers.

Jamie loved being on campus at the start of a semester, a time when the feeling of student optimism was almost palpable. He meandered his way to class, making a wrong turn or two before finding his building and locating his room. Introduction to Professional Development wasn't the most exciting class to teach, but he was happy to be back in the classroom. The course was all about resumes, interviews, and professionalism, which were all things at which many new college students stank.

"Why are you here?" He posed the question to the class.

The class replied with vacant stares.

"Come on, why are you here?" he asked again.

"To learn how to get a job," someone volunteered from the back.

"Well, that's pretty easy. Head on over to the campus burger place and fill out an application. Class dismissed," Jamie said and paused for laughter from the class, but none came. "No, dig deeper. What kind of job?"

"An engineering job."

"Better," Jamie responded. "Why an engineering job?"

"Because that's my major," the student responded as if that should be obvious.

"Why did you choose that major?" he asked.

"I'm good at math."

"Fine, but do you think being good at math is going to drive your entire career? What do you want from your career?" he asked the room.

"Money. I want a lot of money," someone else responded from the back.

The class chuckled. A girl with a long frizzy ponytail slowly raised her hand.

"Yes," Jamie gestured toward her.

"I want to use my skills to do something meaningful or make a difference. I want to do something that will make me happy."

"Great!" he announced with a little too much enthusiasm.

The girl sat back in her chair, regretting her decision to participate.

"We want to do what makes us happy! For some of you, math might make you happy. For others, it might be helping people. Some want to make just enough money to raise a family, and they don't care about the job itself. Most of you fall somewhere in the middle. The time that you'll spend in class over the next five years is going to be valuable but not nearly as valuable as the time you spend outside of class, making friends, interning, and playing one large game of trial and error. This is where you'll figure out what you're passionate about and what to pursue if you put in the effort. This is where you learn that the random opportunities that cross your path will define the rest of your lives, not whether or not you get an A or a B on a physics final. I'm here to help you put some of the pieces together. By the end of this class, you'll have all of the professional tools that you need to secure your very own internship, but more importantly, you'll have a tool kit for navigating all the paths that will appear in front of you over the next five years."

He spent the rest of the class time guiding students through the creation of elevator speeches and having them introduce themselves. That was a tall order for a group of nervous freshmen, but he was impressed by their enthusiasm. After class, he met up with Sarah at a restaurant across the street from campus.

"How'd the first day of class go?" she asked while trying to gracefully take a bite of her sloppy meatball sub. It wasn't working.

"I think it went well. It's an easy A for most kids, so most don't take it very seriously, but I can usually grab one or two. Did you teach today? I've never even asked what classes you teach," Jamie said, eager to change the subject away from himself.

"US History 1 this semester," she replied. "I teach two sections of one hundred fifty or so. It's a big lecture class, and it covers everything up through the Civil War." The way Sarah spoke about the class made it apparent that it wasn't her favorite to teach. "What is it that you teach, exactly?" she asked.

"Cincinnati's class is a bit different than what I taught in Pittsburgh, but it's basically a professional development class that prepares students for internships. We talk about resumes, interviewing, goal setting, stuff like that." He took a bite of his hoagie.

"Sounds interesting. Hey, I've been meaning to ask: would you want to see a movie on Friday?" she asked. "There's a new indie flick that's playing at the little theater near your house. It looks pretty good. There's also a really cool Irish pub that's over in that direction. I know it's an odd recommendation, but the inside of this place is amazing, plus the owner's authentically Irish, as in he was born there and has the accent and everything."

He thought for a moment. "I found a whole collection of old movie reels in one of my uncle's bedrooms. We could go out and see something, or we could go back to my place and hook up his old projector. It's not exactly as fancy as an actual theater, but it could be fun. We could just order pizza."

"That sounds great," she said as she tapped her phone to look at the time. "I have to head back to the office for office hours, but how about we meet up around six?" She wrapped up the remaining half of her sub and slid it back into the plastic to-go bag.

CHAPTER NINE

J AMIE PULLED THE SUBARU UP to the gate, rolled down his window, and grabbed the mail from the mailbox. He threw the mail onto the passenger seat and drove up to the house. Buttons was staring out the living-room window, faithfully awaiting his owner's return.

"Hey buddy," he said, fending the pooch off with one hand and trying to keep him from jumping all over his dress pants. He tossed his keys onto the table next to the front door and flipped through the envelopes. "Let's see what junk we have today." He tossed a few of the letters in the trash and ran his finger along the inside crease of a bill to open it. The paper sliced into his finger, and he winced in pain. He tossed the remaining stack of envelopes onto the entryway table and ran up to T.J.'s office to find a letter opener.

Sunlight cast a brilliant sheen on T.J.'s mahogany desk. It had a set of cabinet-style drawers at the bottom and three skinnier ones that ran along the top. Jamie searched the bottom drawers but found no letter opener.

The top-left drawer was locked, and the other three were filled with odds and ends, but no letter opener was in those either. He jiggled the handle of the locked drawer, thinking perhaps it was jammed and could be shimmied loose. It didn't budge, so he bent down to get a good look at the face of it. The carved flourishes were beautifully intricate, but he couldn't see a keyhole anywhere.

"How could it be locked, then?" he said under his breath. He opened the cabinet below the locked drawer and ran his fingers along the underside of it but felt nothing. Jamie stood up and took several steps backward. The surface of the desk was covered with three black leather panels recessed into the wood. The wood itself looked to be hand carved, and it reminded him of the president's desk in the Oval Office. He walked around to the other side in search of some way to unlock the top drawer.

Then he saw it, a small notch in the wood along the left leather panel. It was just big enough to slide a finger into. He hooked his finger underneath the leather panel and pulled, lifting it away from the desktop. This exposed the smooth wooden surface underneath, as well as a small metal latch. He lifted the latch and tugged the handle of the drawer, which slid freely out of the desk.

A sealed file envelope was the only thing in the desk drawer. Jamie pulled it out, unraveled the fastener, and dumped its contents out onto the desk. At the top of the stack was a newspaper clipping, yellowed with age. It was an article about a house fire where two parents and a little girl perished. An image of a smoldering pile of ash, where a large home had once stood, sat next to the text.

"The investigation is ongoing, but police believe that the fire was caused by an overturned oil lamp," he read aloud. He thought back to *Satan's Song*. *Could T.J. have gotten his inspiration for the story from this fire?*

The envelope also included a large aerial photo of a neighborhood. One of the houses was circled in red marker. He held the newspaper clipping next to it, but the image was too grainy to tell if it was the same place. He flipped the photo over to look for a date. The date "9/4/89" was stamped in the bottom-right corner of the photo, but something else was also written on the back of the photo, a faded phone number scrawled in pencil. He pulled his cell phone out and snapped a picture of the number then set the picture aside to see what else was in the stack of papers fanned out on the desk.

He found a smaller clipping of an obituary. It must have been for the little girl who'd died in the fire. She was smiling cheerfully at the camera. Her plaid bow matched her dress, and her curly hair hung down over her shoulders. The similarities between the fire and T.J.'s book were eerie.

Jamie didn't have a paper copy of *Satan's Song*, but he knew Sarah did. She was supposed to come over later to watch movies, and he thought the newly discovered mystery might be a fun way to end the evening. He pulled out his phone and sent her a text, asking if she'd bring over her copy of the novel.

The media room was a bit of a mess, so Jamie spent the afternoon getting it into shape and sorting through old film reels and VHS tapes. He set a few movies aside as likely contenders for the night's viewing. A file box of old screenplays sat behind a stash of framed movie posters. He pulled them out and read through the titles. Most were films he'd never heard of, but a copy of the screenplay for *The Shining* sat in the middle of the stack. *Sarah's going to lose it when she sees this.* He set it aside and continued on his journey to the bottom of the box. The title on the very last screenplay was immediately familiar to him. He pulled out the loosely bound pages of the screenplay to *Satan's Song.*

Jamie set all the movie gear up in the media room, which he fashioned into a drive-in theater of sorts, with the help of an old white sheet. The small projector, which he'd found at the bottom of a closet, appeared to be functional although he'd never used one before. He brought some popcorn home from the store and filled an old champagne chiller with ice and a few bottles of soda. All in all, he was pretty pleased with himself. When Sarah arrived, the look on her face validated all his hard work.

"This is so awesome! What are we going to watch?" she asked.

"I found an old copy of *Suspiria.* Have you seen it before?"

"Dario Argento, right? I love that movie!" she replied.

"I thought we'd follow it with *Don't Look Now.*"

"Sounds great! What do you need T.J.'s book for?" she asked.

"I was going to wait until after the movies to show you, but let's go downstairs, and I'll explain while we wait for the pizza," he replied.

They sat on the back patio and examined the contents of the envelope.

"This sounds exactly like the story in *Satan's Song*, doesn't it?" he asked from across the table.

"I haven't read it in a while, but it does seem really familiar," she replied. "What else was in the drawer?"

"Look for yourself," he said, dumping the contents of the envelope onto the patio table. He shuffled through the papers and slid the aerial photo over to her.

"Where did it happen?" she asked.

"New Haven, Connecticut, according to the article," he replied.

"So T.J. must have taken his inspiration from the fire. The oil lamp was the cause of the fire in the book too, right?"

"Yeah, the cause of the real fire was exactly the same as the cause in the book. It's just too similar to be a coincidence, but there's something else that I have to show you too. I was digging through a few boxes today, and I found a screenplay for *Satan's Song*. I'm thinking that all of this could be related to the script. Maybe the objects in the cases are just props and marketing material."

Jamie wasn't sure what it all meant. *Was any of it real? Did T.J. steal the news story and use it as his own? Why would he keep all this locked up?* He thought back to the suicide note.

```
I'm surrounded by the death and
destruction that I've created.
```

Could this be what he was referring to?

Sarah grabbed the article from the table and pulled her copy of *Satan's Song* from her purse. She flipped it open to the cover page and skimmed.

"This fire happened in 1991," she said.

"So?"

She held out the page for Jamie to read and pointed at the publication date.

"1989, but that's two years before the fire," he said.

"Exactly! He published the book two years before the fire."

"But that isn't possible. The situation was identical."

"Maybe it is all part of some sort of promotion for the movie," she said.

"So it could all be fake? But why would he go through the trouble of keeping all this locked up? Why create all of this stuff without making the movie?"

"I'm sure that studios did it all the time," she replied. "There are so many moving parts to making a movie that it's easy for things to fall through. Maybe T.J. just didn't like the screenplay, or there wasn't enough financing to make it."

"There was something else that I forgot to mention," he said, reaching for the aerial photo. He flipped it over and held it up for her to see. "Maybe whoever's on the other end of this number can tell us something."

"What? You mean you've had a mysterious phone number the whole time, and you haven't called it yet? You have to call it right now," she said.

"It's getting late. Let's just wait until tomorrow," he replied.

"Give it to me, and I'll call. I can't wait until tomorrow." She attempted to snatch the photo from him, but he pulled it away.

"Okay, okay, I'll call," he said, pulling his cell phone out of his pocket.

He typed in the number, set the phone to speaker, and placed it on the table. As they waited for someone to pick up on the other end, the doorbell rang.

"Crap, it's the pizza," he said. "Could you go grab it? I paid for everything online, so it's taken care of."

"But—" she started.

Jamie replied with a pair of sad puppy-dog eyes.

"Fine, but fill me in when I come back." She trudged off into the house.

She returned a few minutes later, holding the pizza box, a few plates, and napkins. "Well?" she asked.

"The guy who answered lives in New Haven, the city where all of this apparently went down. The story is real, and he was pretty excited to hear from me. I think that he might make for an interesting visit. How would you feel about a road trip?" He realized it was a bit presumptuous to ask her on a road trip, someone who'd only been back in his life for a short time, but the words had already left his lips, and he couldn't take them back. "We could throw everything in the car and head to the east coast over the long weekend."

Her eyes widened as she uttered an emphatic yes.

With a bit of fiddling, Sarah was able to get the projector working again. She'd had to use one before when doing background research for a book chapter she'd been writing. She dimmed the lights after leveling the image on the screen.

Jamie hadn't been to the movies since Lilly's death, but this makeshift theater brought back all the memories. The smell of fresh popcorn and artificial butter made him think of his father. As a kid, he'd spent hours watching spaceships and superheroes zip across the screen with his dad while he sipped soda and shoveled candy into his face as quickly as he could. After his dad passed, he would have to plead with Lilly to go, and they only went a few times a year. He would never admit this to anyone else, but whenever he and Lilly went together, he sometimes pretended his dad was with them and had simply gotten up to get a snack from the snack bar. For a split second, he could sometimes convince himself that he was still alive.

Later that night, Jamie and Sarah sat together in the darkness of the theater room as images flashed on the improvised projector screen. That was strange for him, bringing someone new into an experience that had been so full of emotion. However, something about Sarah eased his apprehension and made him feel as though he were taking a deep breath and letting all the pain and anxiety go, at least momentarily. They had created a temporary world that consisted solely of each other, the film, and Buttons, who lay at their feet, enjoying the occasional piece of rogue popcorn.

CHAPTER TEN

THE PLAN WAS SIMPLE. THEY would drive to meet the contact in New Haven on Saturday morning and uncover the truth behind the documents locked away in the desk. If they were lucky, they would be able to glean some additional information not in the newspapers. A logical explanation for everything probably existed, but the excursion would still make an interesting story for later.

Jamie loaded his and Sarah's travel bags into the car, along with a few snacks and dog food for Buttons, who ran around the yard, soaking in the last bits of glorious freedom before the long car ride. They would take a handful of small highways until they reached 95 then drive up the coast into New Haven.

Sarah thought making breakfast sandwiches for the road would be fun, so she was standing in the kitchen sorting through various sizes of biscuit cutters to use as forms for the fried eggs. The dog had picked up the scent of bacon from the yard and was staring through the window of the kitchen door.

"They're almost done," she called. "Do you want cream in your coffee?"

"No thanks, just black, please. Everything's ready with the car. Can I do anything to help?"

"How about a hand with carrying everything out?" she replied.

The gate closed with a clunk as the Subaru pulled down the driveway, and the little devil child watched the car pull away. Jamie had grown accustomed to the figure, perched on top of the gate, and liked to think it protected the house while he was away.

"So what do you think about all of this?" she asked.

"The fire and everything? It's crazy," he replied.

"No, I mean this." She made a sweeping gesture toward the surrounding trees and Turner House. "Did you ever imagine that you would live in a place like this?"

"To be honest, there was a time when I couldn't imagine what I would have for breakfast." He smiled.

"Why do you say that? Because of your uncle's death, you mean?"

"No, I really wasn't that close to him. The last year or so has been pretty rough."

"I didn't mean to be nosy. I'm sorry. We definitely don't have to talk about it if you don't want to." She looked over at him then down at her lap.

"It's totally fine. You can be nosy," he replied. "It's all still so surreal. Lilly died a little over a year ago, and I was living in a cookie-cutter apartment, surrounded by reminders of everything I'd lost. All that I wanted to do was go home, but there wasn't a home to go to. We sold Dad's house after he died, and that's where I grew up. I went from having everything that I could ever want to having nothing within a year or two."

He realized he'd taken the conversation to a dark place pretty quickly, but Sarah didn't seem to mind and listened intently. He looked over at her and noticed a tear swelling in the corner of her eye.

"But things have definitely gotten better," he said. "A year ago, I couldn't have imagined that I'd be pulling out of my mansion to go on an adventure with someone who's pretty cool." He turned his head and smiled at her. He was afraid he'd unloaded too quickly, but the words all came rushing out before he could stop them. It was true—he'd felt a welling sense of optimism over the past few days. He'd thought his story would end with him curled up in a ball in his apartment, but fate seemed to have other plans. He was just thankful to have one more go at things, at life. His life wasn't what he'd imagined, but it was still life all the same.

It seemed Sarah wasn't sure what to say, so instead she placed her hand on top of Jamie's, which rested on the gearshift, and gave a sympathetic squeeze.

They passed extravagant houses of various shapes and sizes on their way out of town, each filled with families all creating stories of their own.

Some, like Jamie's, were filled with tragedy and loss but all intertwined in some way.

Buttons made a bed for himself out of a few old blankets in the back of the car. He stared lazily at the landscapes that shot by and drifted into the distance. Jamie noticed Sarah sitting in the passenger seat, letting the wind guide her hand up and down, just as he had done as a little kid. They flew down the road blaring Iggy Pop, David Bowie, and the Animals, all from a playlist Sarah had made.

"Did you ever see *Labyrinth*?" she asked.

"You mean starring David Bowie's crotch?" he replied. "It was one of my favorite movies as a kid."

"It's fantastically terrible."

They went through the roster of their favorite eighties movies, and the heated discussion occupied them for nearly half the drive. Jamie threw Buttons the occasional treat and stopped the car every few hours to let him stretch his legs and do his business in the grass. They stopped at a truck-stop diner for dinner and talked about their game plan over burgers and fries. The dog sat in the back of the car and scarfed down his usual kibble.

"When do you think we'll get to New Haven?" she asked.

"Probably around nine or ten. We're going to meet the mysterious man behind the phone number tonight," he replied.

"Where's that?"

"I want it to be a surprise. I think that you'll like it."

"Ooh, a surprise," she said between bites of her burger.

They topped their meals off with pieces of pie and ice cream, which they agreed were practically mandatory when eating at a diner. Buttons lay in wait, hoping they'd remembered to bring him something special for his patience and undying loyalty. He jumped for joy when he saw the little to-go bag in Jamie's hand.

Getting to the mystery locale took a few more hours, but they managed to make it just as the sun went down. They pulled onto the main drag of what appeared to be a one-road town and drove by a small movie theater and a few family restaurants.

"We have arrived," he said, pointing at a storefront that had an iridescent glow from several bright neon signs.

Sarah read them aloud, in no particular order. "Museum of Intrigue. Real Monsters Here. Live Mermaid."

For some reason, the "Live" was no longer illuminated.

"Thought that you'd like this place. There aren't many like it left. For some reason, they have a hard time staying in business," he said, squinting from the bright lights.

"I can't imagine why." She giggled.

"The guy who owns it is Sebastian. It was his number, and he's been here for years," he said.

Jamie parked the car in front of the museum, and they headed inside. Buttons stared from the back window, once again left to entertain himself. The bell on the screen door jingled as they opened it, and they walked over to the vacant cash register. They must have been in the gift shop. The items on the shelves were dusty, as if no one had touched them in ages, and the room was decorated with faded sideshow posters. Sarah and Jamie stood there as a bearded lady and a strongman stared down at them.

"Are you sure that it's open?" she asked.

"Didn't you see the Open sign out there?"

"Not unless it was bright and neon."

"It's definitely open." He tapped the bell next to the cash register.

They waited for a few minutes but heard nothing.

"Hello?" he shouted.

A crash, what sounded like tumbling boxes, came from behind a red velvet curtain, which must have hidden the valuable oddities from the eyes of nonpaying customers. The curtain came to life as the flustered curator slid it out of the way with a broom handle.

"Welcome to Sebastian's World of Intrigue," the man said as he made a grand sweeping gesture with the broom.

"Hi, Sebastian," Jamie said, extending his hand. "We spoke on the phone."

"Oh right! Jamie. It's nice to meet you in person. I assume you'll want to see the full exhibit while you're here?"

"Absolutely," he said as he pulled his wallet from his back pocket.

Sebastian shook his head and refused to take the money from him. "It's just good to have you here," he said.

However, Jamie insisted on paying since the place looked like it could use the business.

The curator punched several keys on an old mechanical cash register and pulled a lever to open the cash drawer.

"Here are your tickets," he said as he ripped the ticket stubs. Jamie had a feeling that the shop was a one-man operation, so he wasn't surprised that Sebastian was also the ticket taker.

The man jumped from behind the counter and tottered over to the curtain, which he opened with another dramatic flourish.

"Enjoy. We're closing in a few, but I'll be here all evening. I'll check in on you in a little while," he said as he turned back toward the counter.

The shifted curtain revealed a doorway that led to a much larger room. Sarah and Jamie were greeted by a skeleton holding a sign with an arrow pointing to the left. It was one of those anatomy-class skeletons, hanging from wires and sporting a removable skull cap of sorts.

"He seems like an interesting guy," she whispered as they walked past the skeleton.

"Apparently, he's been running this museum for a few decades. There still must be a market for odd roadside attractions."

The two made their way through the exhibit, which had a striking resemblance to T.J.'s collection at Turner House, although slightly shabbier and less authentic. They passed a Fiji mermaid, which appeared to be half a fish and half a monkey, the skeletons glued together. Jamie could see the glue lines.

"So the number on the back of the photo was Sebastian's?" she asked while peering into a display box of shrunken heads.

"Yeah," he replied. "I called it, and he picked up. He was the one who sent the info on the fire to T.J. and was pretty eager to meet and talk about it."

Sebastian caught up with them while they were perusing a casting of Bigfoot's footprint.

"So how do you like the exhibit?" he asked, a glint of pride in his eyes.

"Everything's great," Sarah responded, hoping her overenthusiasm seemed believable.

"How long has the museum been here?" she asked.

"I started it in the nineties. At the time, it barely filled the front of the building. I used to live in the back until my collection became so large that I had to expand," he said with pride. "You two must be pretty tired if you've been driving all day. How about I make some coffee and take you to my office, where

I keep my research. After all, that's why you're here, right?"

"Sounds good," Jamie said.

"Just a second. Let me lock up the front of the store."

Sarah mouthed the word "research" as Sebastian walked away. Once he was fully out of earshot, Sarah leaned over and whispered in Jamie's ear, "I'm relatively certain that this guy isn't an axe murderer who uses his victims in his creepy exhibits, but something about him seems off."

When she looked at Jamie for reassurance, he simply responded with a shrug and mumbled, "What do we have to lose?"

Sebastian locked the front door, flipped the Open sign off, and turned the lights off in the front room. "Follow me," he said.

CHAPTER ELEVEN

EBASTIAN LED SARAH AND JAMIE to a pair of olive-green bookshelves, which held a collection of preserved sea creatures, all neatly jarred and labeled. He grabbed the sides of one set of shelves and grunted as he struggled to pull it aside. It was set on casters guided by small metal rails set into the floor. As he pushed the bookshelf aside, a wooden door slowly revealed itself.

"Mind giving me a hand with the other one?" he asked, red in the face and breaking a sweat.

Jamie grabbed the other bookshelf and braced himself to push it out of the way. Either the man's small stature or his lack of exercise must have been to blame for his struggle because Jamie found the shelf to be much lighter than it appeared.

"Thanks," Sebastian said while wiping his forehead with a handkerchief. "That used to be a lot easier."

"Why the hidden door?" Sarah asked, apparently still assessing whether or not Sebastian might actually be a threat.

"It keeps the customers from snooping around. I was always fascinated by trapdoors and secret compartments as a kid, so it was one of the first things that I built when I started the shop."

Jamie looked around at the empty room and dust-covered shelves. He doubted that snooping customers were a big problem.

Sebastian turned the brass knob on the door of the secret room. "This is where I store all of my research."

The room itself was a small broom closet, no more than a few feet wide. The walls were lined with photographs and news clippings. Jamie was reminded of something from a network detective show, with red bits of string connecting the various pieces of evidence. *This must have taken years of work.* He noticed a copy of *Satan's Song* sitting on Sebastian's desk. It was in tatters, as if it had been read hundreds of times. Pages were dog-eared, and sticky notes protruded in every direction. The front cover had been taped back on.

"So what's the connection between the book and the actual fire?" Jamie asked. "We found a movie script and figured that all of this might just have been a big marketing ploy."

"Oh, not at all," Sebastian replied. "I grew up down the street from the actual property. It was the best-looking house on the street when I was a kid. Over the years, it fell into disrepair, and the neighborhood kids even said it was haunted. We didn't know the old guy who lived there, but the new family had to completely gut the place after they bought it. I was in my twenties when it burned down, and I'll never forget it. I was a volunteer firefighter at the time. Everything, and I mean everything, in that house was destroyed. We did what we could, but there was no way that we could have saved them. The building started to crumble, and we had to pull out. I remember standing in the yard, watching everything collapse as ash fell from the sky like snowflakes. I could hear the other neighbors standing behind the police tape, talking about how the family was so kind and the little girl so sweet," Sebastian trailed off. "And then I found the music box."

"Wait, you mean you found an actual music box in the fire? We thought it was a prop," Jamie said. He thought back to the ending of T.J.'s novel.

Everyone and everything in the house was completely destroyed, all except for a wooden music box pulled from the smoldering rubble.

"It was sticking out of a pile of debris as if it had floated to the surface. The light from the fire must have hit it just the right way, and it caught the corner of my eye. It was in perfect shape. Even though it was made out of wood, there wasn't a single burn or scratch. I couldn't leave it there."

"So you stole it?" Sarah asked.

"Not exactly my proudest moment. I felt like it was asking me to take it," he replied.

"How did T.J. get it, then?" Jamie asked.

"I held onto it for years until I stumbled upon *Satan's Song*, a few years ago. I can still remember how I felt when I read that last line of the book. I thought about telling someone, but who do you tell about a possessed music box that makes people kill? People already thought that I was a loon, but I didn't want them to think that I was cashing in on a tragedy as well."

"Not to be blunt, but how do we know that this isn't the case?" Sarah asked. "I mean, the family had different names from the characters in the book, and music boxes aren't exactly hard to come by."

"Sarah, wait," Jamie said.

"No, this is nuts. Clearly, he just made a box that looks like the one described in the book. Anyone could do that."

Sebastian turned toward her. "If you're suggesting that I fabricated the music box, what makes you think that I didn't start the fire as well?" he asked matter-of-factly.

Jamie wasn't sure how to take Sebastian's odd response, but his mind could easily piece together a story where the man was an arsonist whose obsession for T.J.'s book had driven him to murder. He eyed the door, but Sebastian stood in front of it, blocking any means of escape. After a few deeps breaths, Jamie had fully convinced himself that he was being paranoid.

Sebastian continued. "Once I read the book, I sent a package to T.J.'s publisher with the music box and everything that I knew about the fire."

"What happened after that?" Jamie asked.

"Well, nothing for a year or two. Then one day, out of the blue, I received a message from T.J. on the shop answering machine, thanking me for sending the box and assuring me that he believed me. He was going to fix it, he said."

"Fix it? What did he mean 'fix it'?" Jamie asked.

"Not sure, since I never had the chance to talk to him directly. He didn't leave a number in the message, and the call was listed as a private number. Didn't find out about his death until you called," Sebastian replied. "So you found all of my stuff locked up in his desk drawer?"

"All of the evidence, I guess. The box itself is locked up next to the other object…" Jamie had been so focused on the music box that he had forgotten all about the film reel.

"What do you mean other object?" Sebastian asked, a note of worry in his voice.

"The movie reel, you know, from his second book," he replied.

"You mean this happened again?" Sebastian asked.

"I guess so. I haven't found anything about the movie reel. To be honest, I'd completely forgotten about it."

"Do you know anything about your uncle's second book?" Sebastian asked.

"Nothing, besides that it's about some sort of haunted movie," he replied.

"I've got a copy upstairs that you can have. If you two want to wait in the gift shop, I'll go grab it," Sebastian said, teetering toward the door.

Sarah and Jamie walked through the exhibit and into the gift shop while Sebastian disappeared around the corner.

"What do you think about all of this?" she asked. "This guy is clearly a little obsessed."

"Not sure what to think right now. I think that I need to sleep on it. If all of this with the music box is real, if he actually found it in the fire, then I wonder what that means for T.J.'s other book. If there's a story behind the box, then there's probably something to the film reel too," he said.

"You don't know anything about it?" she asked.

"Not a thing. Granted, there's no telling what other stuff is hidden in that house. I'm sure that we've just scratched the surface."

"Here." Sebastian handed Jamie a copy of *Cellulose*, which was much less tattered than his copy of *Satan's Song*. "You'll want to read this."

A question had been forming in the back of Jamie's mind. His better judgment told him it was absurd, but he decided to ask anyway.

"If the box is supposedly possessed, did anything strange ever happen when you had it? It's such a powerful force in the story, but you just slipped it into a package and mailed it off to T.J.?"

"Nothing," Sebastian replied. "I had it for a long time before I even knew about *Satan's Song*, and not a single thing happened. I'll admit, I was a bit creeped out after I made the connection, but that was it. You two keep me posted if you find anything."

Buttons was sleeping peacefully in the back of the Subaru. Jamie felt bad for having left him in the car for so long, but the night was cool, and he seemed to enjoy the time to himself.

The trio booked a room in a hotel nearby. After smuggling the dog inside, Jamie went back out to pick up dinner. When he returned, the hotel door creaked loudly, and it seemed to startle Sarah, who slammed her laptop shut as he entered the room. He set the bags on the table and headed toward the bathroom.

"Going to take a quick shower, but don't wait for me," he said, shutting the bathroom door behind himself.

Jamie held his head under the shower faucet and let the warm water run down his body. The water pressure was terrible, but the temperature made up for it. The day had been long, and he was happy to have a moment to himself to process everything. Although Jamie wanted to believe Sebastian was just a crazy old man and the contents of the envelope were somehow related to the movie script, he couldn't shake the nagging feeling that he and Sarah had stumbled upon something darker.

CHAPTER TWELVE

AMIE FORKED A PIECE OF his egg in a basket while Sarah appeared to be staring off into space.

"My mom used to make these for me all the time when I was growing up," he said to break the silence.

"Huh?" She snapped back to reality.

"Have you ever had these before?"

"You mean a toad in the hole? I used to make them all the time in college," she replied.

"Toad in the hole? That name doesn't make any sense." He laughed. "Are you okay? You haven't said a word for fifteen minutes now."

"I did a bit of research while you were out getting dinner," she said. "I have all of the documents from T.J.'s envelope scanned into my laptop. When I pulled up the old newspaper clippings and read through them again, I noticed something I hadn't before, a name. I did a web search, and it turns out that the girl's family still has one relative in the area, her father's sister. Her name's Mary, and she lives on the coast, up the highway a little ways.

I gave her a call this morning. She wasn't exactly thrilled to talk to me on the phone but agreed to meet nonetheless. I wanted it to be a surprise."

The Sunday-morning air was cool, and the diner where they were eating was filled with chatter and the sounds of clinking forks and coffee cups.

Sarah and Jamie finished their breakfast and headed back to the car with a side order of scrambled eggs for the dog. The car pulled out of the gravel lot and onto the road as the clouds rolled in over the coast. The weather was cool and dreary, but Jamie's optimism was swelling in his stomach. He knew he was getting closer to something although he wasn't sure what it was.

"Did Mary know anything about the book?" he asked.

"She didn't seem to. I'm hoping that she'll at least remember the music box. That would lend some more credit to the story. I still don't trust Sebastian. The guy gives me the creeps."

"He's definitely a little different, but even if we throw his story about the box out the window, the fire definitely happened."

"Did you ever stop to think that maybe he really did start the fire? He even brought it up. I think that he's a little out to lunch," she said.

"You're right. That's why we have to find proof that the girl had that box before the fire. Mary just might be able to provide that."

Jamie thought that, at the very best, they'd prove that this was all some sort of hoax. At the very worst, they had uncovered a murderer. However, even if Sebastian had had something to do with the situation, it was still a pretty big coincidence that the house was nearly identical to one described in the book, as was the cause of the fire.

Jamie parked the car next to the entrance of the condo building. He had a strange feeling in the pit of his stomach, a sense of foreboding made worse by the dark clouds seeming to spill out from behind the tall brick building. Sarah brought the dog leash around to the back of the car. The ride up the coast had taken an hour or so, and Buttons was eager for a potty break.

They walked the stone path through the courtyard and up to the front door. The courtyard was well manicured, with neatly groomed shrubs and carefully etched flower beds. The entryway sat between four large pillars, which held up an intricately carved pediment. Mary hadn't given the impression of affluence over the phone, but this place likely reflected the wealth of its tenants.

As Jamie and Sarah admired the details of the building, the entry door swung open.

"Good morning," said the doorman. "You must be here to see Mrs. Cohen."

"Indeed we are, sir." For some reason, Jamie felt the need to speak with unnecessary formality.

"She mentioned that you'd have a furry friend with you," the doorman said as he looked at the dog and smiled.

"Mind if I... ?" The doorman pulled a dog biscuit from his pocket.

"No, not at all," Jamie responded.

"Here you go, sir. Mr. Buttons, is it?"

The doorman knelt to hand the treat to him, and he graciously accepted it with all of the regal attitude that a dog could muster. His tail wag made it clear he liked the guy.

"I'll take you to the second floor." The doorman gestured inside.

He guided them through the entryway to the elevator. The three of them stepped inside, and the doorman reached around and hit the second-floor button.

"Once you exit the elevator, take a right. It's suite two oh nine. Mrs. Cohen is expecting you."

"Thank you," Sarah said as the doors slid closed.

"What a nice place," Jamie said. "Mary must be loaded!"

"She could have fooled me," she replied. "She was so nice on the phone. I pictured her in a tiny little cottage, sipping tea and surrounded by cats, my kind of lady."

Once the elevator doors opened, Jamie and Sarah turned right and walked down the hallway. They stopped at door 209. Jamie looked at Sarah, trying to discern what she was feeling. She smiled and tilted her head toward the door as if to say "go ahead." He knocked lightly and stood back.

The iron doorknob jiggled, and the door opened slowly.

"Hello there," Mary said with a bright smile, popping her head outside the condo. "Come on in. I was just boiling some water for tea."

At least Sarah had been right about the tea.

Mary swung the door open. She was wearing a plaid poncho with warm colors that matched her crimson corduroy pants and large red spectacles. Her hair was pure silver and wavy, pulled back into a short ponytail. The condo was a colorful reflection of her wardrobe, with bright paintings of abstract shapes hanging in the entryway. The walls were painted a sunny yellow.

"What are those?" Sarah asked, pointing at some miniature trees sitting in the corners of the room.

"Those are money trees," Mary replied.

"I didn't know those were real things," she said.

"Of course, that's in name only. They're from Central America. The little trunks are braided together when they're saplings so they grow into a giant braid. I've had these for years."

They walked down the hallway, and Mary steered them into the kitchen. The hanging cabinets were painted aqua while the counter cabinets were a dark purple. They sat at the kitchen table, which was topped with colorful ceramic tile.

"Would you like some tea?" she asked, pulling the kettle off of the burner.

"Yes, please," Sarah replied.

"That would be great," Jamie said.

Mary set two cups on the table and went back for the third. Jamie lifted the tea cup to his nose.

The tea smelled moldy. He wasn't an expert, but he was pretty sure tea wasn't supposed to smell like old library books.

"This smells great!" he lied. "What kind is it?"

"Oh, I should have told you beforehand. It's pu'er tea with a bit of ginger. It's basically fermented Chinese tea leaves, and the fermentation process gives it an earthy smell. I drink it all the time, but I forget that it's an acquired taste."

He was pleased to find the tea didn't taste nearly as bad as it smelled, and the ginger masked the earthy notes.

"Have you been to China?" Sarah asked, cautiously sipping her tea.

"Several times. I taught English there once before it was fashionable. I still go back every now and then for pleasure," Mary replied.

"Wow! Did you go to teach while you were in college or something?" she asked.

"I was forty-two at the time. My husband had just passed away, and I thought that my life could use a little adventure. It was the first time that I'd left the country."

"That must have been nerve-racking," Sarah said.

"It was. But then it wasn't. I'd always thought of myself as too timid to travel, but after my husband's death, I realized that life was too short to be afraid. It turns out that the big bad world isn't really so big or bad once you get to know it."

Mary appeared to be many things, but timid certainly wasn't one of them.

"So you're here to talk about the fire?" Her expression changed as abruptly as the topic.

"We have some questions, if that's okay," Jamie replied.

"Certainly. I can't promise that I'll be able to answer them since it was a quarter of a century ago, but I'll do my best."

"We've been doing research on the history of New Haven, for a film project that we're working on." Jamie figured this sounded better than "We think a cursed music box killed your family."

"We found out about the fire while sorting through some old newspapers at the library and were wondering if you knew anything about the house that your brother lived in," he continued.

"Not much, unfortunately," Mary replied.

She explained that the family had purchased the old Victorian home with the hope of restoring it to its former glory. The girl's name was Emily, and her father, Steven, had been a high-profile lawyer in Chicago. He moved to New Haven after his mother had a stroke and began the slow march toward death. He had worked hard all his life, but his mother's stroke helped him to realize his work often came at the detriment of his relationships with his family. The job in New Haven was a simple one and would allow him to be close to his mother while rebuilding his life with his wife and daughter.

"Emily loved that house," Mary said. "She'd wander around with a flashlight, exploring all the old cabinets and hiding places. Her parents forbade her from going into the attic or the cellar, but she made a game of hiding in the nooks and crannies around the house. She'd wait for her parents to walk by and jump out to scare them."

"It sounds like the house was in disrepair for some time. Who lived in the house before them?" Jamie asked.

"I think that he was a retired priest. He lived there for years, but the place really started to fall apart in the few years before his death. He must have been in his mideighties when he died. Had a bit of a drinking problem too, judging by all of the empty bottles left scattered around the house."

"Did he die in the house?" he asked.

"I believe so, but it wasn't anything dramatic. He fell asleep one night and never woke up. It took a few weeks for someone to find him, at least based on what the neighbors said. He was an odd fellow," she replied.

"What made him so odd? There are a ton of alcoholics out there." Jamie had a few in his family.

"Well, for one, he bricked up the basement door," Mary replied.

"Why would he do that? To keep people from breaking in through the basement or something?" Sarah prodded.

"I have no idea, but he also covered the bricks with a giant painted cross. I've always found the devoutly religious to be a bit odd anyway, but this was something different. There was trash all over the second floor, but the ground floor was pristine. It looked as if he lived on the second floor and never set foot on the first."

"Do you think that he was scared of the basement?"

"Could have been. Steven had a hell of a time cleaning everything up. The bank sold the house as is, so they left all the junk behind. He took time off to start the cleanup prior to moving his family in."

"This might sound like an odd question," Jamie said, "and I'm sorry to bring all this back up, but—"

Mary cut him off. "Darling, I've been through my share of tragedy. I've had a few decades to make my peace with losing them, so don't you worry."

"Did Emily ever go down to the basement even though she wasn't supposed to?" he asked.

"She was a smart girl. If she wanted something, she would get it. I don't recall that she was ever in trouble for going into the basement, but she was pretty good at hiding her misdeeds." Mary held her teacup with both hands and stared into the swirling liquid.

"Have you ever seen this before?" Jamie asked as he slid his phone across the table.

Mary adjusted her glasses, picked up the phone, and held it at arm's length, trying to find the sweet spot where the image on the screen came into focus.

"Where on earth did you find this?" she asked as her expression soured.

"Someone sent it to us. They claimed that it was recovered from the remains of the fire."

Jamie felt uneasy about leaving out all the details. Mary had been nothing but nice to him and Sarah, but he didn't want her to know about Sebastian, at least not yet. Being confronted with an artifact from a tragedy was one thing, but he didn't see any point in confronting her with the far-fetched story of why they were there in the first place.

"It looks like Emily's music box. She kept it on her nightstand and listened to it when she went to sleep."

Mary paused as if trying to piece together the details of the story that she was about to tell. "I stayed with her one night while her parents had gone to a friend's house for a party. I tucked her in, and she asked to listen to the music box, so I left it open. I must have fallen asleep on the couch for an hour or so while I was reading my book. When I woke up, I went upstairs to check on her. I could still hear the music box, so I figured that she had fallen asleep. As I got closer to the door, I could hear her whispering like she was talking to someone. At first, I was frightened, so I barged in and flipped on the light. Of course, she must have been talking to herself, but I scared the living daylights out of her. She jumped up and slammed the music box shut. I felt terrible about it, so I laid with her until she fell back asleep."

"Are you sure that it's this box?" Sarah asked.

"I think so, but it was so long ago. I remember talking to Emily about how pretty it was. It had carved leaves on top, with some sort of pattern etched in the front of it. It definitely had the same dark finish." Mary sat back in her chair with a vacant expression, as if reliving the moment with her niece. Sarah and Jamie sat in silence, not wanting to take the moment away from her. "I would love to have it when you're done with your project. Would that be okay?"

"Of course," Jamie responded.

Mary was quiet and somber now, and the color seemed to fade from their surroundings as a cloud passed overhead.

"Thank you so much for coming, but I hope you won't mind if we wrap up. My energy's just been zapped right out of me. Please let me know if I can do anything else to help," she said as she pushed the chair out from the kitchen table and stood up.

Buttons, who'd been sleeping underneath it, stood up and stretched his legs across the tile floor.

"Thank you so much for your time. It was great to meet you, and sorry to dampen your day," Sarah said.

"Don't worry about it. I'm a resilient old bat," she replied with a grin.

Jamie loaded the dog into the back of the car while Sarah opened the passenger door and climbed in.

"I wish that we had brought it here," she said, fifteen minutes into the drive.

"Why?"

"Maybe if we'd brought it with us, we could have made sure that it was the same one."

"If Mary isn't absolutely sure that it's the same one from the picture, seeing it probably wouldn't help." He paused. "But hearing it might. Maybe she'd recognize the song. If it mentioned the song in the book, maybe she'd remember if it was the same one."

"But the book doesn't mention the song specifically. We'd have to find the keys to that case and see for ourselves," she said.

The visit seemed to confirm Sebastian's story, but it only led to more questions. One of T.J.'s fanatical fans, likely Sebastian, could have set the fire to pay tribute to the book, but the coincidences were too many to ignore. T.J. had clearly written the book before the fire, and the actual fire, the family, and everything involved were nearly identical to the story. *What does this mean?* Neither one of them could fathom the possibilities. Not only did they have to confront the box when they returned, but they hadn't even scratched the surface of the film reel, the other object in the display cases. *Did* Cellulose *have some twisted connection to reality as well?*

CHAPTER THIRTEEN

T HE SUBARU PULLED UP TO the iron gate of Turner House, and Jamie hopped out of the car to push it open. He was glad to be home, back under the protective gaze of the young devil. For some reason though, home felt a little less like home than it had before. Although he had grown used to his uncle's odd collection, and it was starting to feel like a collection of his own, the eerie circumstances surrounding the objects in his uncle's library made him wish those objects were somewhere else, at least until he could figure out what was happening.

"Do you want to come in for a minute?" he asked Sarah as she reached for her bag.

"I'd love to, but I have an early class tomorrow morning. I should be headed back," she replied.

"Okay. I hope that you enjoyed our little adventure," he said with a smirk.

"It was definitely more than I expected," she replied. "I can't wait to see where it goes from here. You're fun to adventure with," she said as she leaned in for a hug.

Sarah walked to her car, and Jamie drove down the gravel driveway toward the house. When he looked in the rearview mirror, he noticed she had stopped and was looking back at him.

Once inside, Jamie flipped the light switch in the front entryway, but nothing happened. The house was completely dark. He walked into the living room and tried the switch there—nothing. He stepped out onto the front porch. The streetlamps were shining brightly, and the lights were on in the houses down the hill. *I must have blown a fuse.*

Finding the fuse box took some time. He scanned back and forth along the basement wall with his cell-phone flashlight and finally located the box at the far end of the basement. Buttons stood close by his side, visibly frightened by the groans and creaks coming from the recesses of the cellar. Instead of a breaker he could simply switch back on, Jamie was confronted with outdated plug fuses. He scoured the shelves next to the fuse box, searching for spare fuses, but came up empty-handed. The junk drawer upstairs also provided no help. The problem was well beyond his capabilities to fix tonight.

"Great. Well, looks like we're roughing it for the night. I'll stop by the hardware store in the morning to grab some fuses," he said to the dog, who tilted his head as if attempting to understand his master.

Jamie started a fire in the living-room fireplace and spread a few blankets on the floor. Fortunately, he could still use the gas stove, which could be lit with matches. Dinner consisted of stovetop popcorn and a can of soup, not exactly a feast, but that was all he could motivate himself to make. Buttons lay in front of the fire, positioning his body so that it could absorb as much heat as possible. Sebastian's copy of *Cellulose* stuck out of Jamie's bag, but he wasn't ready for another mystery, at least not tonight. Instead, he explored his uncle's bookshelf and pulled out a hardcover book about Ireland. The pages contained hundreds of images of rolling hills, small villages, and stone houses.

The night reminded him of his first night in the old apartment. He, Lilly, and the dog had camped out on the carpet, looking through magazines and watching movies. Now it was just him and the dog, but the feeling was the same, as if he had just moved in, and in a way, the house felt new and foreign to him.

"Sarah would have loved this," he said to Buttons.

A feeling of guilt washed over him. He'd meant to say Lilly's name, but Sarah's came out by mistake. However, he did want Sarah to be here, to share this moment with them. Ever since Lilly's death, he'd been in a haze, a haze that had slowly started to lift over the past few days. Sarah had brought a new sense of adventure to his life, and the ongoing mystery gave him purpose. Instead of pure self-satisfying fascination, he felt a sense of duty to some larger force in the universe to figure things out. Part of him was also afraid of what he might uncover. He didn't fear being harmed or anything like that, but a tiny space in the back of his mind was terrified of finding more stories of pain and suffering that validated the presence of something sinister. *What if Sebastian was telling the truth, and the events of T.J.'s book did happen two years after it was written? What if Sebastian had had something to do with it?*

Restoring power to the house took several days. Jamie assumed the issue had been a blown fuse, but actually, a fallen tree had ripped the power line from the back of the house. He made the most of the situation and invited Sarah over for a day of feasting. They cooked the most valuable perishables in the fridge, and she packed the rest up in a large cooler, to hold them at her place until power was restored. Buttons also benefited from the outage and had eggs with a few bites of steak. Going back to kibble would be hard.

Jamie busied himself by searching the house for the key to unlock the glass display cases. If he could free the music box and identify the song, he might be able to tell once and for all whether or not it was Emily's. He scoured T.J.'s desk drawers and examined every inch for evidence of secret panels or compartments, but he found nothing. Jamie searched the entire library from top to bottom and found nothing. He turned the bedroom upside down, looking in nightstands, wardrobes, and closets—still nothing. Although his search for a key was fruitless, he did find a hammer in the stairwell leading to the basement. At this point, he was willing to break a little glass if that meant he would be able to put the music-box mystery to rest.

The display cases appeared to be made of domed glass and sat on a recessed shelf in the wall. They were held down by a wooden frame that slid over the lips of the domes and was secured by a single lock. He held the hammer up and considered the potential ramifications of his actions. He wasn't afraid of a little broken glass. Rather, he feared releasing whatever demon lived inside the box. *That's stupid.* He shook off his fear, reminding himself that no such things as demons, curses, or supernatural things existed, and he swung.

The hammer ricocheted off the dome, sending painful vibrations up his arm. This clearly wasn't glass. The loud *clunk* made Buttons leap into the air and run from the room. Jamie swung again as the dog peered around the doorway. The hammer hadn't even scratched the dome's surface. He tried breaking it a few more times, but his hand became number with each swing. He sat in T.J.'s desk chair and wiped the sweat from his forehead.

"Guess we're not getting in without a key," he said as Buttons approached cautiously, now that the hammer was safely on the desk. Jamie slumped in the chair and pressed his hand against his forehead. A key had to be somewhere. He thought back to the desk drawer with the secret lock. The key could have been anywhere, hidden in some secret recess of the house.

Unless.

He felt a slight glimmer of hope and pulled his phone from his pocket. He tapped Don's phone number in his contact list and held the phone to his ear.

"Hi Don, this is Jamie Lawson. When we settled my uncle's estate, you mentioned a safety-deposit box. Did you ever find the key for it?"

CHAPTER FOURTEEN

G IANNINI BANK AND TRUST WAS an austere
limestone building that sat near the city
center. Jamie pulled open the heavy glass
doors and stepped inside. The bank was even more
impressive on the inside, with incredibly tall ceilings
and spotless marble floors. Don had needed a few
weeks to sort out the safety-deposit box access with
the bank since T.J. was the sole owner. Although
Jamie was now the owner of the box on paper,
the key was nowhere to be found. The bank would
have to drill through the original box and replace it
with a new one, all on Jamie's dime, of course. He
checked in at the front desk, and the receptionist
verified his identification. She picked up the office
phone and tapped in the extension with her long
fingernails.

"It'll be just a moment, sir. Please help yourself
to some coffee or a Danish while you wait." She
gestured toward the coffee bar.

He stood in the waiting area and sipped his
cup of coffee for a few minutes. Idleness gave his
mind time to run over all the possible outcomes of

the day's visit. *What if the key to the object cases is actually in the box? What if we can prove that the box was actually Emily's? Does it prove demonic possession or possibly that Sebastian recreated the story and murdered the family? And what if the box is empty? Where do we go from here?*

"Good morning, Mr. Lawson," said the bank manager. He was tall and lanky and wore a fitted pinstripe suit with a red handkerchief tucked neatly into his breast pocket. "Shall we make our way down to the vault?"

"That would be great," Jamie replied, pulled from his endless loop of what-ifs.

"I'll just need your signature on this form, which gives us permission to drill through the deposit box and signifies your agreement to pay for its replacement."

He handed Jamie a pen, and he scribbled his signature on the form. Then they took the elevator down to the vault level, accompanied by a maintenance man carrying a large drill.

"It must be pretty difficult to drill through a deposit box," Jamie said.

"By design," the man replied. "We use one of the best boxes in the industry, so it takes quite a drill bit to break one of these open."

"If I might make a recommendation, it's a good idea to document the location of your keys, in case you would like to pass the box down in the future. As you're aware, it's quite a hefty cost to replace the box," the manager said.

For a moment, Jamie imagined his untimely demise.

"I'll definitely do that," he replied, pushing the image from his mind.

"Here we are, sir," the manager said, gesturing for him to step out of the elevator.

Two guards stood on either side of the vault door, which was wide open. A door made of steel bars, similar in appearance to a jail cell, separated the contents of the vault from the outside world. The manager removed a large key ring from his pocket and examined each key one at a time until he came upon the correct one. He opened the steel door and led them inside.

The manager nodded to the maintenance man, who located the box on the wall and began the excavation process. The door to the box was very small, about the size of a standard legal envelope. As the man steadied his drill on the lock, the manager pulled out a pair of earplugs from his pocket and pressed them into his ears. The sound of metal eating away at metal was terrible, and the manager seemed to be hiding his displeasure with it behind a contrived smile. *No wonder replacing the box is so expensive.*

Jamie's palms were sweating as his anxiety had kicked in with full force. If the box held anything else besides the key to the cases, he'd have no idea where to look next.

"There we go," the maintenance man said as his drill bit tore through the last bits of the lock. He cleared out the hole and tapped the latch with a hammer, freeing the box from the wall. He set the small box on the viewing table.

"We'll leave you to your box. Please let me know if you need anything. Once you're finished, please place any items that you do not wish to take in the new box." The manager gestured toward a new deposit box on the table. "Just lock it up, and we'll put it away for you. The keys are in the box lock. I've included a copy, as you requested." The manager left the room with the maintenance man close behind.

Jamie held his breath as he flipped open the metal lid. This was the best chance he had at finding the key that would open the object cases.

A skeleton key sat perfectly in the middle of the velvet-lined box, held in place by two metal pins. An intricate floral design made the key handle while the teeth were complex rectangular shapes. This was what he had been looking for.

The box lay empty on the table as he placed the key in the front pocket of his messenger bag. He locked the new deposit box and rang the bell. One of the vault guards led him back to the main lobby, where he signed out at the front desk. As he left the building, Jamie pulled out his phone and tapped Sarah's face in the speed-dial menu.

"Any luck?" she asked, having answered after a single ring.

"I found a key," he replied. "I can't believe it. I think that this is it!"

"You found it? That's great!" she said.

"I'm on my way back. How about you head over in a few. We'll crack open a bottle of wine and try it out?"

"Already headed out the door," she responded.

"See you soon."

Jamie's heart pounded with each step. He'd expected to find old bonds or jewelry, maybe even gold bars, but he hadn't actually expected to find the key. It was all that lay between him and the music box.

CHAPTER FIFTEEN

S ARAH STOOD UNDER THE PORCH light, which cast an eerie shadow on her face. She held a large paper bag in one hand and an umbrella in the other. Clearly, the tiny travel umbrella had been no match for the unexpected shower, and the rain and strong wind had twisted and contorted it into a tangled, wiry mess.

"I managed to make it three-quarters of the way up the drive before my umbrella collapsed," she said as Jamie greeted her at the door. "Let's get this party started," she added. "I hope you like soggy burritos." She held up the wet brown paper bag and smiled.

"My favorite!" he replied. "Let me take the dog out, and we'll see if we can open the cases."

Buttons was already waiting at the back door. He ran out to do his business as quickly as possible but was soaked by the time he returned to the porch.

Sarah grabbed a few dishes out of the cabinet and plated the food while Jamie uncorked one of the bottles of wine on the table.

"I'll take the plates upstairs, and you grab the wine," she said. "Buttons, how about you weave in and out between my legs and try to make me fall down the stairs?" He was more than happy to oblige, and Jamie followed close behind.

Jamie took a few bites of dinner then retrieved the key from his bag. Sarah looked on eagerly, sitting on the edge of T.J.'s desk.

"Here goes nothing," he said as he inserted the key into the case.

The lock mechanism shifted as he turned the key. Sarah took a deep breath. The wooden frame was heavy but lifted out of the way with a bit of extra force. With the frame out of the way, nothing else was holding the domes in place, or at least that's how it appeared. Jamie tried to lift the lid of the music box's case, but it still wouldn't budge. He pulled as hard as he could, but it seemed to be cemented in place.

"Maybe twist it. Leftie loosie?" Sarah said, trying to be helpful.

He gave the dome a forceful twist to the left and nearly fell over as it spun around easily and lifted off. He placed the dome on the ground, and they stared at the box, unwilling to approach it.

"You know, if all of that demon stuff is true, we're probably pretty stupid to touch it," he said.

"You don't actually believe in that, do you?" Sarah asked.

"Of course not, but still... If this is Emily's music box, it means that the fire happened just as it had been written in the book. So, what does that say about the box?" He thought it was a fair question.

"Well, I'll keep you from burning the house down if it comes to that," she replied.

He had come too far to let the chance of demonic possession get in the way. In truth, deep down, a part of him was terrified. He stepped forward and flipped open the lid to the music box. Nothing happened.

"You have to wind it," she said, her cupped hand muffling the sound of her voice.

Jamie flipped the box over and found the winding mechanism. He gave it a few twists then righted the box. The chimes came to life as the sound echoed through the house. He stepped backward, nearly tripping over Buttons. The song was an obscure one, something he'd never heard before.

"Recognize it?" he asked.

Sarah listened for a moment. "I don't. I was expecting something common like something from *Swan Lake,* but I have no idea what song that is."

"Do you still have Mary's number?" he asked.

"Already pulling her up," she replied.

Jamie heard a quiet voice through the speaker of Sarah's phone.

"Hi, this is Sarah. We're back in Cincinnati, and we have the music box with us. If we put it up to the phone, could you tell us if you recognize the song?"

She must have agreed because Sarah walked over to the case and held the phone up to the music box.

The line was silent for a moment. Mary said something, then Sarah thanked her and hung up the phone.

"This is it. It's the music box from the book, and Mary says that Emily played the same song. Sebastian is telling the truth," she said.

"This is the box," he reaffirmed as if trying to convince himself. "So what do we do now?"

"I think that we should have another movie night," she said, pointing at the film reel. "If all of the stuff with the music box really happened, we've got to check the film reel."

He agreed with her but felt needles forming up and down his spine. This was becoming a little too real to be entertaining, and he didn't know if he could handle another tragic story. *If the music box was cursed, then what about the reel? If the people in T.J.'s novel went mad when they watched it, then what would happen to the two of us? However, even Sebastian said he'd never experienced anything out of the ordinary with the box. There's got to be a logical explanation for this.*

The makeshift movie screen was still in place from the other night, as was the reel projector. Jamie took the film tin from the object case and carefully pried it open, revealing the film reel inside. He hadn't read the second book in the *Dreadful Objects* trilogy yet but wasn't sure he'd be able to bring himself to watch the film if he knew the sinister history behind it. The reel was still holding together, but it was significantly worn. Sarah had shown Jamie how to use the projector the other night, and he set it up while she looked on anxiously.

The reel spun to life as it fed through the projector, and the blank frames flickered on the screen.

A large white art deco house came into focus, the camera appearing to have been placed in the street. They watched for several minutes as the sun slowly set over the house although nothing else in the frame changed. The owner flipped on the first-floor lights, then the second-floor office lights came on. Jamie could make out the figure of a woman taking a seat in the office. She appeared to be working at a desk, and several minutes passed without incident. The camera sat perfectly still as the woman typed away in her chair.

The frames flickered and faded as if the film had been damaged. As they came in and out of focus, the lamppost in the front yard pulsed. The bulb flashed and went out as the frame came back into perfect focus.

The film appeared to be burned as a dark spot appeared in the middle of the frame. It slowly took shape, a shadow positioned as if it were standing on the sidewalk. But the shadow began to move independently from anything else in the shot. It floated up the front walkway of the house and to the front door, which swung open. The lights on the first floor all went out at the same time, flashing in the same fashion as the lamppost. Both Sarah and Jamie jumped.

The woman on the second floor appeared to hear the door but quickly returned to her writing. A minute or so went by before the light in the upper bedroom went out, and the woman disappeared into the darkness.

The shadow emerged from the door and slowly floated down the sidewalk toward the camera. Jamie felt uneasy as the entity came closer to the camera, once again affecting the quality of the frame. The frame grew white hot, and the image of the house was swallowed by light.

But it wasn't the figure causing the tremendous amount of light on the screen or a burning smell, for that matter. The film was actually too close to the bulb and caught fire, projecting a boiling pattern on the screen.

"The film's on fire," Sarah said, bolting to her feet and running to the projector.

"No, no, no!" Jamie shouted as he tried to douse the fire with what remained of his glass of water. No luck. "Get some more water!" he shouted as he grabbed the reel of film and ripped it off the projector. The body of the reel started to catch as he flung the film into the fireplace. As the film caught, a tornado-like flame shot up from the center of the reel.

She came back with water but stared helplessly at the blazing film reel. They had no hope of saving it, but fortunately, Jamie had managed to get it to the fireplace before it consumed the entire house. Buttons backed himself into a corner and barked.

"Are you okay? Did you burn yourself?" she asked, walking over to examine Jamie's hand.

"I'm okay," he replied. "What the hell was that? Was it coming for us?" he asked.

"No, it was just the film material. That stuff is super flammable. It's why they stopped using it," she replied. "What do we do now? It's completely ruined."

"1859 Resor," he replied.

"What?"

"The address on the light post was 1859 Resor," he said.

Sarah grinned, hugged Jamie as tightly as she could, and kissed him on the cheek.

Clearing the room of smoke from the fire took the better part of an hour. They opened all the room's windows, set up a few box fans, and blew the smoke outside. Although the smoke quickly dissipated, a haze remained.

"So why is that stuff so flammable? It was terrifying, wasn't it?" he asked.

"It's old nitrate film. They used to make all movies with the stuff, but eventually it was replaced by safer materials. There was a film warehouse fire a few decades ago where thousands of reels of film went up in flames, and a dozen or so were the last remaining prints of movies that were lost forever. It's nasty stuff."

Jamie appreciated Sarah's geeky level of historical knowledge at moments like this. He grabbed his laptop from the living room, and they turned the kitchen table into a mobile command center. Typing "1859 Resor" into the search engine led him to a local news-archive site.

"Come look at this," he said, pulling up a news article. "Eighteen fifty-nine Resor burned down on October 2, 1999."

> Fire officials are investigating the cause of a fire that destroyed a Cincinnati home on Saturday, claiming the life of one of its occupants. Initial investigation points to faulty wiring as the potential cause; however, this has not been confirmed. Louise McAulle, a local film critic, was at home at the time of the blaze and was unable to escape.

Jamie found the obituary in the results list.

> Louise is survived by her husband, William, and son, Gregory. Donations may be made to the McAulle family at St. Stephen's Church on Clinton Avenue.

"That's only a few blocks from here. This doesn't make any sense," she said.

Jamie had a sickening hunch. He reached across the bar, pulled the copy of *Cellulose* towards him, and thumbed through to the pages.

"Nineteen ninety-seven. The book was published in 1997. It came out two years before the fire."

CHAPTER SIXTEEN

BUTTONS CLEARLY SENSED SOMETHING WAS up. Jamie grabbed his jacket from the coat hook and laced up his sneakers while Sarah took the breakfast dishes into the kitchen. This typically only meant one thing: they were going to go for a walk. Buttons spun around on the entryway carpet, grabbed his leash from the table next to the stairway, and laid it at Jamie's feet.

"Okay, bud, hold on a second," Jamie said, patting him on the head.

While Buttons continued to spin on the carpet, Jamie jumped up from the couch and switched the living-room lights off. Sarah grabbed the leash and snapped it on the dog's collar, then they headed out the door.

Resor Road was only a few blocks away from Turner House, in a weird twist of fate that Jamie didn't quite understand. They'd had to travel all the way to the East Coast to find the truth behind T.J.'s first novel, but the events of the second had occurred a mere four or five blocks away. *How could this be?*

Buttons tugged aggressively on the leash. Although he was leash trained, he clearly couldn't repress his excitement for long walks and all the smells that came along with them. Sarah and Jamie discussed the second novel on their way to the street. Getting to New Haven had taken hours, but they were standing in front of 1859 Resor Road within fifteen minutes of leaving the house. At least, they were standing in front of where 1859 Resor Road used to be. He assumed that the house would have been rebuilt and that new occupants would be painting a joyful picture over the previous tragedy. Instead, they were confronted by a vacant lot. It had been cleared of debris and appeared to have been mowed recently, but the house had never been rebuilt.

"That's odd. I can't believe that it's been nearly two decades and no one bothered to rebuild here. This property must be worth a fortune in this part of town," Jamie said.

Indeed, land prices in the area had skyrocketed as the university grew and brought more and more people into the city.

"I wonder if the McAulles still own the land," he said. "Maybe it was too painful for them to rebuild here. We'll have to do some more research when we get home."

"Stay here. I'll be right back." Sarah marched up the stone walkway of the house next door and rang the doorbell. A deep bark echoed through the halls inside, but none of the human inhabitants were home. She walked over to the house on the other side of the lot and tried the doorbell. Just as she started to turn away, the door opened a crack to reveal a wrinkled face.

Jamie and Buttons watched as she chatted with the elderly woman, who gradually opened the door to reveal her hunched frame. The woman closed the door and went inside. Sarah turned and smiled at Jamie, giving him a thumbs-up. She stood at the doorway for a few minutes, then the woman reappeared. She handed Sarah a small slip of paper, which she accepted with a slight nod and a thank you. She turned and headed back to Jamie while the woman waved at him. He returned the wave although he was unsure of exactly what was going on.

"What was that all about?" he asked.

"Remember Gregory from the obituary? This is his number," she said as she handed him the scrap of paper. "Her name is Molly. I told her that you were my husband and we were moving to the area. I mentioned that we were wondering who owned the lot next door because we would be interested in buying it."

"You're brilliant!" he said with a smile. "Did she tell you anything about the family?"

"She just mentioned the fire. The father didn't handle the stress of it very well. Greg was away at college at the time, and his dad, William, wasn't mentally stable enough to live by himself anymore. He quit his job and moved into an apartment nearby, and Greg stopped by now and then to check on him. She still talks to him every once in a while, but apparently he moved his dad to an assisted-living home a few years ago."

"What about the lot? Why haven't they rebuilt?"

"She didn't say. Obviously, someone in the family pays for its upkeep, but she hasn't seen Greg in years."

"It sounds like we should give him a call," Jamie said.

They stopped for coffee on the way home. Sarah stood outside with the dog while Jamie went inside. The café owner was pulling a shot at the espresso machine, her curly gray hair bouncing as she turned her head to acknowledge him.

"What can I do for you, dear?" she asked as the espresso machine squealed and hissed.

"Just a dirty chai and a cappuccino," he said.

"It'll just take a minute. I'll meet you at the register."

"Thank you," he said but was drowned out by the screech of the machine.

He stood at the register and took in the sights while waiting for the coffee. Record sleeves were pinned haphazardly to the wall. A smattering of artwork, ranging from finger paintings to small masterpieces were all available for sale. "Friends don't let friends drink Starbucks" was painted in a curly script over the register. The place reminded him of his uncle's house, strewn with collectibles and artifacts.

"Here you go, sweetie. That'll be seven forty-nine."

Jamie slid his credit card out of his wallet and passed it over the counter.

"Thanks. This place is great! How long have you been here?" he asked.

"It's been about twenty-five years or so," she said.

"You know, I was just reading about a fire that happened a few blocks away, a little less than twenty years ago. There was a film critic that lived over on Resor Road who passed away. Did you know her?" he asked, playing the dumb out-of-towner.

"McAulle, wasn't it? She came in here every once in a while to write. I think her name was Louise. We ended up renting out our space at night, once or twice, so that she could host film nights. She got a little weird towards the end but was a nice lady. I didn't know her well, but it's always a shock when someone you know dies. That was a while ago, though." She paused. "That's kind of a morbid thing to be reading about. What piqued your interest?"

"I just moved to town and was reading up on local history," he replied.

"Ah. Whereabouts? This is a great place to live," she said.

"Turner House, actually. My uncle owned it and passed away recently. I'm here to settle his estate and am living there until I can figure out what to do with it."

"I was going to recommend taking a walk up in that direction. It's a beautiful house. He was an author, wasn't he?"

"He was—a horror author, actually," Jamie replied.

"Well, he was definitely living in the right house for that. Anyway, have a nice day. Hope to see you again," the owner said, handing him his card and receipt.

He smiled and nodded, grabbed the coffees, and turned toward the door. He handed the cappuccino to Sarah and headed toward Turner House. He hadn't thought about it while he was speaking with the coffee shop owner, but he wondered what she'd meant when she said Louise was "a little weird" toward the end. He filed that away for later, when they talked to Greg—that is, if Greg wanted to talk.

CHAPTER SEVENTEEN

J AMIE PRESSED HIS INDEX FINGER on the number pad of his cell phone, striking each number with purpose. He placed the phone on speaker and set it on the kitchen island. It rang once... twice... three times. The robot message clicked in, and he left a voice mail in a tone indicating his disappointment that no one had picked up. He hoped the number was right but had no way to tell. All they could do was wait. Fortunately, Jamie had a book to read, and Sarah had assignments to grade.

"Listen to this," she said, reading from a paper on her laptop. "'Benjamin Franklin was a cool guy. He put a key on a kite and invented electricity. He wrote a lot of stuff too and had wooden teeth.'"

"Someone in college wrote that? Are they all that bad?" Jamie asked. He was sprawled out on the couch with Buttons nestled between his legs.

"Fortunately not. Most students at least read the Wikipedia article before they write their papers. It looks like this guy typed this out in ten minutes.

He didn't even bother to run spellcheck." She scrunched her nose as her eyes scanned the page.

Jamie thumbed to the first chapter of *Cellulose*.

> None of the members of the night crew had ever heard a scream of pure terror before, but it was a sound that would haunt them all for the rest of their lives. Although their heads told them to run, their hearts told them to help. The two men sprinted toward the office and burst through the door. The auctioneer sat at his desk, slumped over a stack of inventory paperwork. One of the workmen shook him on the shoulder, but he didn't budge. He pushed the man back in the chair, revealing a lock of such horror on the auctioneer's face that the man recoiled. The official medical reports would show he'd had a massive heart attack, and while this may have been the official cause of his death, the cleaning men would always say that the man died of fright.

Jamie's heart pounded as he finished the opening paragraph. The story wasn't particularly disturbing, but knowing *Satan's Song's* eerie connection to reality left him wondering whether all of this actually happened too. The story went on to describe how Louise obtained the film. Louise had a different name in the book, of course, as did the other members of her family. She purchased the film at auction a few weeks following the death of the auctioneer. It was part of a box of old film reels she'd found at an estate sale. She collected vintage films and would regularly host community viewings and discussions. Although she acquired many films over her years of collecting, something in this innocuous cardboard box would lead to her death.

Sunday morning turned to afternoon as Jamie made his way through his uncle's novel and Sarah finished grading. They'd just finished a late lunch when the phone rang. He was shocked that Greg had even bothered to return the call, especially since he was so forthcoming in his voice mail message. He had mentioned that he was T.J. Lawson's nephew and that the call was regarding a film reel he'd recovered from the items left to him in his uncle's will. He figured his uncle must have retrieved the reel from someone in Greg's family, and Louise's son had probably either known of its existence or actually given it to T.J. Jamie had no idea whether Greg knew the film was tied to his mother's death.

Greg must have been in his midforties, but his voice was that of an old man. He barely remembered giving away the old film reel years before. Everything had been destroyed in the house fire, but his mother happened to have stashed the reel with a few others in a case in her office at work and was planning to send them out for restoration. His dad couldn't bring himself to throw away the contents of her office since they were the only artifacts that remained of his wife, so he stored them in the spare bedroom of his apartment. Greg received a call from T.J. a few years after the fire, claiming he'd met Louise at one of her community filming events and lent the film to her for background on a piece she'd been working on. According to T.J., the film was of substantial sentimental value, and he'd hoped it might have been spared in the fire. That was a lie, of course, but he was clearly eager to prevent the film from doing any more damage. Jamie left that bit out of his conversation with Greg.

"Out of curiosity, did you happen to watch the film?" Jamie asked, playing along with his uncle's long-established ruse.

"Nope. All of mom's films were pretty delicate, and I probably would have damaged them if I tried to watch any of 'em. Your uncle mentioned a marking that was etched into the film reel itself, which is how I found it in the pile."

"Do you know if your mom watched it before she passed away?" Jamie asked.

Sarah sat silently in the background, occasionally scribbling questions for him to ask.

"I'm sure she did, but she never mentioned it. She'd set up the projector in her office and watch them then send the ones that needed repair out to a friend who was pretty talented with that stuff. She never mentioned this specific one, though."

"This might be kind of personal, and you don't have to answer if you don't want to. Did your mom start acting strange at all prior to the fire?" Jamie asked.

"Why do you ask?" Greg replied.

Jamie worried that he'd crossed a line and scrambled to recover.

"Um, my uncle mentioned it. He kept in touch with Louise now and then and said that she seemed like something had been bothering her," he lied. He was sure Greg could see right through him, but he needed to say something. His uncle couldn't have told him anything if Jamie had found the reel in his uncle's estate. The dead can't speak. He hoped Greg wouldn't catch the error.

"I see," Greg said. "We were definitely worried about her at the time. I was at school in Tennessee for most of the year, but Dad mentioned that she'd been acting strangely. He'd catch her muttering to herself every once in a while, and she seemed scattered, not like herself. We thought she might be developing some kind of mental illness, but the fire happened before we could do anything about it."

Sarah scribbled another question on the piece of paper: "Can we talk to his dad?"

Jamie shook his head. The fire had already caused Greg too much anguish, and he couldn't bring himself to rub salt in his wounds by bringing his dad into it. *Could his dad even handle reliving the events?* He thanked Greg for his time and apologized for bringing up bad memories. As Jamie tapped the phone screen to end the call, Sarah exhaled as if she had been holding her breath the entire time.

The call established a few things. Greg knew about the film and had given it to T.J., but he must not have known it was the subject of the book. The music box came to T.J., but he sought out the film. He must have discovered the connection himself.

"When did your uncle move into Turner House?" Sarah asked.

"It must have been the early nineties. Don mentioned that T.J.'s first book was gaining a cult following, and the publisher just cut him a huge check to write the second book," he replied.

"So he moved in before he wrote the second book? He just happened to write the book about someone who lived a few blocks away?"

"You think he knew Louise?" he asked.

Greg hadn't mentioned ever meeting T.J., but it was too much of a coincidence that he'd lived so close to the subject of his second book. They knew the film wasn't a family heirloom, as T.J. claimed, but he might have been telling the truth about having met with Louise prior to the fire. *What if he knew her?*

Jamie picked up the phone and gave Greg another call. He asked if any photos existed from his mother's filming nights, claiming that he was hoping to find an image of his uncle for a keepsake. Greg couldn't help since all the photos and mementos of his mother had been obliterated in the fire. The only photos remaining were photos taken by other family members as well as the few framed photos from Louise's office.

"What do we do now?" Sarah asked.

"I have an idea. I've got to get some work done before class tomorrow, but I'll text you when I'm on my way home," he replied.

"Works for me. I need to go to the gym anyway. I guess I'll bid you adieu until tomorrow."

Sarah stood up, and Jamie watched as she grabbed her bag and headed for the door. He wasn't sure where this story would end up, but he was just happy to have her along for the ride. Another pang of guilt hit him in the stomach.

He poured a glass of wine and sat at the kitchen island to prep for the next day's lecture. The topic was career goals, which made him laugh, considering that his current situation hadn't been created through careful planning and orchestration. His career was the haphazard result of random events, misfortune, and a bit of luck here and there. No one ever set out to be an adjunct or the nephew of a famous horror novelist, but that is where he ended up. The original plan was to be an engineer and design aircraft or some other marvel of modern technology. The math came easily, but the passion for inanimate objects was hard to muster. People were simply more interesting. Jamie was an introvert at heart, but something about teaching excited him. His knack for helping others to see through the haze that society placed upon them was what led him there. His disdain for nine-to-five office work was another motivator.

Buttons lay at his feet as he wrapped up the lecture slides and closed his laptop. He went through the living room and turned off all the lights. The figures and creepy artifacts no longer bothered him. They had become a part of his life as had Sarah and Buttons, and it wouldn't be the same without them. He climbed the stairs and walked to the bedroom with the dog at his heels. The next day, he would stop by the coffee shop on the way to work. A chance existed, albeit slim, that the owner had some sort of memento from the film nights. He just wanted to find something to confirm that T.J. knew Louise prior to the fire, and a photograph would do the job.

Jamie switched off the light and tried to sleep. This was all too surreal. The thoughts of what could lie ahead excited and terrified him. Somehow, his uncle had been able to foresee the deaths of these people. But Jamie knew that ghosts and supernatural things weren't real. He knew that, but he had no other explanation.

CHAPTER EIGHTEEN

TRAFFIC WAS HEAVY, AND JAMIE had to circle the block a few times to find a parking place near the coffee shop. He dashed across the road between the pulse of traffic and pulled open the door. The little bell jingled as it hit the doorframe, and a college-age waitress greeted him as she cleared off a table. Jamie joined the end of the line and peered at the menu. The man behind the bar took his order, but the owner was nowhere in sight. He paid for his drink, walked toward the door, then turned toward the woman wiping the table.

"Do you know if the owner is in today?" he asked.

"She isn't in until later, but is there something that I can help you with?" she replied.

"I was speaking with her yesterday, and she mentioned that she used to hold film nights here, years ago. I was wondering if she had any photos that she would be willing to share with me. I'm doing some research for a project, and they'd be really helpful."

"I'm not sure, but if you want to leave your number, I can give her a message."

"That'd be great! Thanks for your help," he said.

"It's no problem. Just write your name and number down, and I'll make sure she gets it." The waitress pulled an order pad and pen from her apron and handed it to him.

He scrawled his name and number and then thanked her again.

Jamie's office at the university was stark in comparison to Turner House. The walls were completely bare, and all that sat on his desk were a few folders and his laptop. His office was simply a holding cell in which he existed between classes. The first two classes of the day went well, but he still had one more in the afternoon. He was hoping to hear back from the owner of the coffee shop but figured the waitress had probably crumpled up the note and thrown it away as soon as he left. He would try again in a few days if he didn't hear anything.

Jamie grabbed a slice of pizza from the campus food court between classes. The buzz from the students served as white noise to help clear his head. He pulled out his phone and opened his conversation with Sarah. They'd been texting back and forth all morning. She'd just had a huge blowup with her mom, and they weren't talking. Although he tried to reassure her that he didn't mind, she'd already apologized to him several times for venting too much. In truth, he was glad she was opening up more about her personal life. They had been spending a lot of time together, but she kept many things close to her chest as did he. He felt that was partially his fault. The wall he'd put up after Lilly's death was reinforced by a year of self-loathing and stagnation, and he worried that Sarah was taking it as a sign of disinterest. He didn't want to admit it—and wasn't sure what it meant—but he'd started to use the ongoing mystery as an excuse to see her.

A voice caught him by surprise. "Um, Professor Lawson?"

"Hey, Kyle, what can I do for you?" Jamie replied.

"Sorry to bother you. I know that you've already had office hours this week, but I had a few questions about the resume assignment due this afternoon. I saw you sitting here so thought I would see if you had a few minutes."

Jamie figured his assignment was in bad shape if he was willing to interrupt a teacher's lunch. "Sure, take a seat."

He slid his food off to the side, and the student produced one of the worst resumes Jamie had ever seen. Working through the assignment took nearly a half hour, and the student's resume was covered in red ink by the time he was finished. Jamie offered an extension on the assignment, and both of them were nearly late to class.

After class, Jamie sent Sarah a quick text and headed to the parking garage. The drive home took only about ten minutes, but it gave him just enough time to listen to a bit of a podcast, this one about cursed objects. He finished the first half of a story about Richard, a doll that tormented his child owner. The boy's parents overheard him talking to the doll and swore they could hear it talking back. Eventually, the little boy grew up, but the doll never left his side.

Jamie didn't believe in ghosts or supernatural things—at least, he hadn't prior to moving into Turner House—but he loved the folklore surrounding mysterious events. Although he believed explaining everything with reason was possible, turning toward logic was getting harder and harder when so many of his recent experiences seemed illogical. He'd spent a lot of time trying to put together a sound explanation for the events he'd been learning about the last few weeks, but he was unable to do so. The fact that the books had been written before the tragedies was irrefutable. Perhaps some fanatic had recreated the happenings in the book, but explaining away the video and the music box was hard. *Did someone plant them? Could T.J. be responsible?*

He pulled the car through the gate to Turner House and parked on the gravel in front of the entryway. Buttons was in the window, jumping up and down and barking with excitement. Sarah arrived several minutes later, and they headed out back.

They sat at the patio table on the back porch, looking down at the subdivision below. She had her feet propped up in a chair, and he fiddled with the fire pit.

"How's everything going with your mom? Did you finally call her?" he asked.

"Yeah, things are fine, I guess. She still didn't apologize, but we'd probably never speak again if I held out for an apology." She paused. "But you've probably had enough of my bitching for one day. Tell me about that idea that you mentioned yesterday."

"You're not bitching at all. I would be mad too. I just wanted to tell you that I stopped by the coffee shop today. I was hoping that the owner might have some photos or something from the nights that Louise held her film screenings."

"Why? Do you think that T.J. was there? He doesn't mention them in the book."

"How else could he have met her without the family knowing anything about him? We know that she inspired the character in the book. It's just too big of a coincidence that a film critic died in a fire blocks away from a novelist who wrote a book about a film critic dying in a fire. He would have had to have followed her or at least researched her, right?"

Sarah watched as a tiny figure appeared from a house below and dragged a garbage can to the curb.

"But that doesn't make sense," she said. "If T.J. followed Louise around and researched her for his book, then how the hell did he know about Emily? I mean, he couldn't have. She lived hours away, and Sebastian was the one who told him about the fire. Clearly, he didn't write *Satan's Song* with Emily in mind."

Sarah had a point, but it only raised more questions and got them no closer to an answer.

The crumpled-up newspaper danced as it was swallowed by the flame. Jamie carefully blew, and the kindling slowly caught as well.

"That should do it," he said as he stood back and admired his work.

CHAPTER NINETEEN

J AMIE OPENED THE DOOR TO the wine cellar and descended the stairs. Buttons watched from the top of the stairs but refused to go down with him.

"Come on, bud. Help me pick out a good bottle," he said, patting his thighs, but the dog responded with a meek whimper and refused to move. "Okay, then. Guess I'm on my own."

The close-your-eyes-and-pick-one strategy of wine selection had served Jamie well, so he saw no point in stopping now. He walked across the hellscape and along the countless rows of bottles, stopping every now and then to examine a label. As he touched the neck of tonight's selection, he heard a dull growl behind him.

"What's wrong? I'll be right back," he said to the dog.

The growl was louder a second time. He turned around, but Buttons was nowhere to be found.

"Where are you? Come here, bud."

The sound was coming from a dark corner of the cellar. *He must have cornered a rat behind one of the wine racks.*

Jamie walked toward the noise, lighting the floor of the cellar with his phone flashlight.

The growl grew louder, and he came to a terrifying realization: that wasn't Buttons. He flipped the flashlight up to illuminate the recesses of the cellar. In a brief flash, the light caught two glaring eyes. A black wolflike creature stood in front of him, baring its sharp yellow teeth. He slowly backed away, toward the cellar entrance, and the beast lunged as he turned and ran full speed toward the stairs. His shoes were sticking to the floor, though, and he struggled to keep a pace fast enough to escape whatever was behind him. As running became more and more difficult, he looked down to find his shoes hadn't been sticking to the floor but rather melting into it.

The underworld scene came alive below him, and steam rose from the hot floor. The demons twisted and writhed underneath his feet and appeared to grow closer as if coming for him. Jamie let out a scream, but no one was there to hear, aside from the creatures in the floor. A hand reached from below and grabbed his ankle, and the sound of hand meeting flesh was the same as a piece of bacon meeting a hot skillet. He was being burned alive. Another hand came for his arm, and Jamie tried to pull away. He let out a second terrified scream.

His cell-phone alarm ripped him from the dream and out of the depths of hell. The sheets were damp with sweat, and catching his breath took several moments.

A voice-mail alert flashed on the screen of his phone, sitting on the bedside table. He picked it up and hit Play.

"Hi, Jamie. This is Cindy from Sunrise Cafe. One of the baristas mentioned that you stopped by. I did some digging when I got home last night and pulled out the old cafe photo albums. I found a few shots from the screenings and would be happy to make copies for you. Just let me know your email address, and I'll send them over."

Jamie hopped out of bed and hit the callback button on his phone as he walked downstairs to sit at the kitchen island. He gave Cindy his email address, and she promised to send the pictures to him within the next few minutes.

Buttons was waiting patiently for breakfast, so Jamie put a scoop of kibble into his dog bowl before flipping the coffee pot on. He opened his laptop as the coffee pot came to life, the dark elixir slowly trickling down to the empty vessel below.

A quick refreshing of his email revealed no new messages. He grabbed a mug from the kitchen cabinet and poured a cup of coffee before returning to his computer to refresh the page again—still nothing.

After several minutes of rapid refreshing, an email with the subject line "Photos" appeared at the top of the queue. Jamie hovered the mouse pointer over the email, but something felt off.

He typed out a message to Sarah. *She has them.*

A reply came several minutes later. *Who has what?*

She emailed the scans of the pictures from Louise's screenings. Are you free? I'll send them your way.

Sarah called within five minutes of Jamie sending the text.

"I'm going to forward the message to you now," he said.

"All right, but hurry. I've got a committee meeting in twenty minutes," she replied.

Three images were attached to Cindy's email, one from 1994 and two from 1996. He opened the first and pored over it, with Sarah doing the same on the other end of the line. Louise, or at least a woman he assumed was Louise, sat next to a collapsible screen and projector cart. She was pointing at something on screen, and he could barely make out the image of two figures sitting in front of a cloudy sky on the coast. A chess board appeared to be sitting between them.

"What's on the screen?" he asked.

"It's *The Seventh Seal*," Sarah replied without hesitation.

"The what?"

"She's showing *The Seventh Seal*. That's Death on the left, and he's playing chess with the knight on the right. The knight is playing for his life."

The coffee shop seated twenty or so people, and Jamie continued to scan the image for any signs of T.J.

"Back corner," Jamie said, looking at the seat farthest away from the projector. At first, making out T.J.'s face was difficult since it was slightly obscured by his tweed driving hat, but the round spectacles gave him away. He was sitting in the corner booth and staring vigilantly at the screen.

Jamie opened the next image. This time, T.J. was sitting in the middle row.

Sarah let out a slight gasp on the other end of the call.

"What's wrong?" he asked.

"Look at the last picture," she replied.

In the final picture, T.J. sat front left, directly next to Louise. This time, though, he was glaring at the camera. The light from the flash had caught his eyes, giving them a demonic red glow.

"Oh, that's creepy," he said.

The images proved T.J. knew Louise prior to publishing the novel, but this raised more questions. *How did he know about the film reel and the fire? Did he give Louise the film? Was he somehow responsible? And what about Emily? If T.J. was somehow involved in Louise's death, what about the little girl to whom he had no apparent connection?*

"So where do we go from here? We're out of books, and it looks like we're out of leads," Sarah said.

"I have no idea. Maybe we should start looking into the house. That was supposed to be the third book, wasn't it? Maybe there's something about it," he replied, rubbing his chin. That was a direction, but he wished they had something more concrete to go on. *Where are the mysterious messages to guide me from here? The trail is cold.*

CHAPTER TWENTY

INCINNATI WINTERS WERE UNPREDICTABLE. SOME presented themselves as light chills in the air while others bore down with cold anger. This winter fell into the latter category. The first storm of the season left the roads slick with ice and covered with a deceitful layer of peaceful fluff. The university slid to a halt, as did the cars on the city streets. The school had been closed for three days, an unprecedented number of consecutive snow days, according to Sarah.

The snow was too deep for Buttons. Jamie watched him from the back patio as he did his best to keep his belly from touching the white powder. Jamie made a snowball and whistled to get the dog's attention. He tossed it to Buttons, who jumped up to catch it. It exploded on impact, leaving him confused by its sudden disappearance. Jamie laughed and headed toward the door with the pup close behind him.

"Let's get you dried off, bud," he said as he grabbed a towel next to the door and wrapped it around him.

Buttons moseyed over to his water bowl while Jamie pulled a large stockpot down from the kitchen cupboard. He had tried to convince Sarah they could reschedule their planned winter feast, but she insisted on braving the blizzard. Now he was obligated to deliver and was hoping that baked ziti would be acceptable. It was the last pasta dish in his cooking repertoire, which was in sore need of expansion. He filled the pot with water and set it on the stove to boil, then he went down to the wine cellar to grab a bottle. Ever since the nightmare, he'd forced Buttons to go with him each time he went into the cellar. The dog probably wouldn't be able to save him from an evil wolf demon, but he found it comforting to know that he wouldn't die alone if such a beast were lurking in the corners of the basement.

The doorbell was barely audible from the cellar, but Buttons heard it and turned tail to run upstairs and greet Sarah. *Bad timing.* Jamie quickly grabbed a bottle from a shelf and scurried up the stairs.

Over the past few weeks, things with Sarah had started to change—just stolen glances at first, but he noticed their goodbye hugs had been lingering as well. He met her work friends a few times and was under the impression that she'd told them a lot about him. Maybe he was imagining it all, but part of him hoped he wasn't. He still thought of Lilly every day and wasn't sure what dating again would be like, if he could even bring himself to date again, but something about her made him think it might be worth a try.

Sarah stood at the door with a container of dressing in one hand and a salad bowl in the other.

"How did you manage to ring the doorbell?" he asked.

"The baguette," she replied, wiggling a thin loaf cradled under her arm.

He helped her inside, with Buttons close behind them. The water started to boil over, so Jamie ran to turn the burner down and throw the pasta in.

"Thanks for coming over tonight. Sorry that you had to risk your life to get here," he said from the other room. "We could have done this some other time."

"It's no problem," she said. "It was either dinner over here or frozen dinner alone in my apartment with the cat." She paused. "Wow, I promise my life isn't typically *that* depressing," she added.

Jamie had met her cat, Theodore, on several occasions but wasn't impressed. Apparently, Sarah had taken custody of Theo when her sister moved across the country for a new job. Her sister's new apartment had a policy against pets, especially devil cats with a fondness for human suffering. He was a crummy pet in Jamie's opinion, but Sarah seemed to enjoy his company.

He assembled the ziti and slid it into the oven while she pulled plates from the cupboard and prepared the salad. They ate in the dining room and watched the storm through the windows.

"You interned in Japan, right?" Sarah asked, forking a few noodles.

"Yeah, for about six months or so. It was pretty awesome," he replied.

"What was the craziest experience that you had there?"

Jamie smirked. "There were quite a few memorable moments, but I'd say the time that we missed the last subway train home. A group of us were coming back from a festival, and we sprinted to catch the last train, which ran around midnight. We ended up catching it, but it only went a few stops before they kicked us all off and shut it down. We ended up walking the nine stops home, which took us till sunrise. One of my friends had a little handheld camera, and I actually found some of the old footage on a DVD when I was packing up the old apartment."

"You're kidding! Why didn't you just call a cab? They have cabs in Japan, don't they?" she asked.

"They do, but we were poor college students at the time and a little intimidated to try to communicate with a cab driver. We didn't know much Japanese."

"Would you ever go back there? It seems like such an interesting place. I've always wanted to go."

"Work sent me for a conference a few years ago, but we didn't have that much time to explore. I would love to go back again."

"Well, you just say the word, and I'll go with you," she said, glancing up and smiling at him.

After dinner, Jamie made spiked hot chocolate, and they moved to the living room to enjoy dessert. He walked over to the kindling box next to the fireplace and flipped open the lid to find a match. It was empty.

"Looks like we're out of matches. Let me run upstairs and see if I can find some more," he said.

A matchbox sat on the mantle of the fireplace in the makeshift theater room, but it was empty as well. He went next door to T.J.'s office. It had a small fireplace as well, and he knelt down and found matches in the kindling box. As he started to stand back up, Jamie noticed a partially burned scrap of paper protruding from the ashes. He'd never used this fireplace before, so it must have been a remnant from T.J.'s last fire. He reached in and fished out the piece of paper.

A few typed words remained on the page although the soot made them somewhat difficult to decipher. After wiping as much ash as he could away with his hand, he stared at the paper in disbelief and read it one more time just to be sure it was real.

The hardwood bowed under Jamie's feet. Sarah didn't turn around but talked to him while she scooped a bit of whipped cream from the top of her drink with her finger. "Did you find matches?" she asked.

He didn't respond.

"Did you find any matches?" This time, she raised her voice, as if she thought he had gone into the other room. "Ugh," she said and spun around.

Jamie stood in the doorway.

"What's wrong?" she asked, as she stood up and walked toward him. "You look like you've seen a ghost."

"Read this." He outstretched his hand, offering her the singed piece of paper.

She took the scrap from him and attempted to wipe the remaining ash away, only managing to smudge it with her fingers.

Jamie arrived at Ash and

Sarah scrunched her nose. "What is this?" she asked.

"I found it in the fireplace. Someone tried to burn it but did a crappy job," he replied.

"Who's Ash?"

"That's Don. He's the lawyer that I worked with to finalize all of the stuff from T.J.'s will." Jamie paused, carefully choosing the words for his next sentence. "I did this. I had to go there to talk about the will. It's like someone was following me."

Sarah giggled. "Ha ha, very funny. Stop with the BS. You're making this up," she laughed.

"No... I'm not. I have no idea where this came from. I'm dead serious. I found this in the fireplace."

Her smile faded. She grabbed Jamie by the arm and walked across the room, her heels pounding into the hardwood.

"Where are we going?" he asked.

"To see if there's anything else up there," she replied with resolve.

They climbed the staircase into T.J.'s office. She knelt down next to the fireplace and reached inside, tugging at the metal grate, which still held several charred logs.

"Give me a hand with this," she said after several exasperated attempts to move it.

Without questioning, Jamie knelt beside her and grabbed the other end. The two pulled, and the metal scraped loudly against the stone floor. They slid the grate completely off the hearth, scattering soot and ash everywhere.

"You might want to go grab a plastic bag," she said as she grabbed the small broom from the hanging set of fireplace tools.

Sarah swept around the inner edges of the hearth, scraping bits of unburned debris from its recesses and obscuring the green Rookwood tiles with deep black ash.

"Look," she said as she spread the ash apart with her hands, revealing the edges of a yellow-tinged scrap of paper. They sorted through every scrap left in the fireplace, shoveling the useless stuff into a black garbage bag. One, then two small pieces of charred paper now lay on the tile hearth. Both Sarah and Jamie were covered in soot.

"Whoever was trying to get rid of this stuff did a terrible job," he said.

"It could have been T.J. I mean, if he killed himself, he knew that you'd have to meet with Don at some point. It's probably just a coincidence or something to do with his will."

Jamie wiped off the slips of paper as carefully as possible so as to not damage the typed text. He could make out a sentence fragment on the first piece, which he read aloud.

"It looks like the first one mentions 'a shelf of audiobooks,'" he said.

Why does this seem familiar? Slowly, his brain made the connections. He'd found the copy of the *Satan's Song* audiobook at the gas station between his old place and Cincinnati and had made a huge mess when he bumped into the CD shelf.

"What about the second one?" she asked.

"The metal latch under the leather panel," he said. This sent chills up his spine. Even if T.J. had planned for him to find the latch to the drawer, he was alone at the gas station. No way could anyone have known about both unless...

"Someone's spying on you," Sarah said.

"Someone's been in the house," he said as he felt the hairs on the back of his neck stand up.

That was the only explanation.

"We should call the police," she said.

"From the car," he added.

"How about we stay at my place tonight?"

Jamie shot her a confused glance.

"I mean I have a pullout couch," she added.

He packed up a few things in a small suitcase and locked the doors and windows. Buttons clearly wasn't thrilled to be back in the snow, but Jamie managed to corral him into the car. He followed her to her apartment, a few streets over. The roads were a mess, but her Jeep handled them well. Jamie fishtailed around the corner of the intersection, but no other cars were on the road to worry about. No one was crazy enough to drive in this weather.

The apartment complex was an old U-shaped building with a center courtyard. The front steps led them through a brick archway affixed with concrete letters that spelled out "The Colonel." Jamie wondered who the Colonel was, but he kept it to himself, considering the severe circumstances of his visit. Now wasn't the time.

"Up this way." she directed him down a mazelike hallway, which reminded him of a hotel from a horror movie. The walls were lined with dim lanterns but completely lacked windows. She opened two French doors that led to the large wooden door of her apartment. She let Jamie in, and a little ball of fur darted toward him. He wasn't able to escape Theo's wrath as the cat pounced and clung to his ankle. Fortunately, he was wearing a pair of jeans and had thermal socks on underneath, so the cat's fangs weren't able to penetrate his skin. Theo clearly wasn't happy with the surprise visit. Sarah shooed him away and apologized then grabbed his bag and set it next to the couch.

"You go call the police, and I'll find an extra set of sheets and a pillow," she said.

Jamie wasn't sure whom to call. *This clearly isn't an emergency, but what is it exactly?* He found the nonemergency number for the police and tapped it on his phone screen as he stepped into the kitchen. An unenthused officer answered the phone, and he tried to explain the situation as best as he could without seeming like a complete lunatic. He mentioned that he thought someone was following him and that he believed his house had been broken into. The operator transferred him to the detective's desk, where he repeated the entire story. The detective seemed even less enthused than the operator.

"Are you sure that one of your friends isn't playing a joke on you?" he asked.

"I'm certain. No one else has keys to the house," Jamie replied.

"Look, it doesn't sound like you're in danger. We can't send anyone out today. It's a nightmare out there, and all of our guys are preoccupied, but we can send someone tomorrow or later in the week. In the meantime, it's probably a good idea that you stay with someone else. Call 911 if you see anyone following you."

The detective's nonchalance was somewhat reassuring. If it was a serious situation, surely he would have said so and headed out right away. Jamie thanked the detective and hung up.

"Well?" Sarah asked as he walked back into the living room.

"Looks like I'll need a place to stay for a day or two. Think Theo would mind?"

"Oh, he loves you," she replied.

Theo, in fact, was glaring at him from the chair in the corner of the living room.

CHAPTER TWENTY-ONE

ETECTIVE WILKS SEARCHED THE HOUSE for
more than an hour, checking every corner,
crack, and crevice. Jamie had never met a
detective before, but Wilks was pretty close to the
stereotypical image he had in his head. He wore a
tan overcoat with a blazer and tie, and Jamie tried
hard not to stare at the man's majestic mustache.

"I forgot how enormous this place is," Wilks said.

"You've been here before?" Jamie asked.

"Yeah, I did the investigation when the previous
owner... You know. I gotta be honest with you kid—
if you hadn't mentioned that you were living in this
house, I probably wouldn't have even bothered to
come out. Figured that you were just a nutcase at
first, but given the history of this place, I thought
that I could at least give things a look."

"Well thanks, I guess," Jamie replied with a
bit more snark than he had intended to. He was
surprised by the lack of enthusiasm but was also
relieved to have the detective give the place a
once-over.

Buttons was relegated to the backyard for the duration of the search and displayed his dissatisfaction with the intruder by barking at him through the window of the back door.

Despite a thorough search, the detective came up empty-handed. No more scraps of paper were in the fireplace, nor were any signs of breaking and entering visible.

"This house is empty, son," he said. "If I were you, I'd invest in a security system, at least for the peace of mind."

"I appreciate you coming out here. Sorry to waste your time, Detective," he stretched out his hand and met the detective's with a firm grip.

"No problem. Like I said, I have a history with this place, so it's good to see it in good hands. I never met the first guy, but he seemed like a weird dude, at least based on what he left behind."

"I know. This collection is unreal, isn't it?" Jamie said.

"Yeah, that's for sure, but that journal takes the cake," Wilks replied.

"What do you mean? What journal?" Jamie was confused.

The detective thought for a second. "You know, there's a good chance that no one ever came back to claim it, so it's probably still in our evidence locker. We conducted a small investigation when your uncle passed, just to make sure that it was actually a suicide. You can never be too careful with people who have any amount of celebrity—they tend to attract some odd folks. We collected a few things, but they didn't help us too much in the end. If I remember correctly, we found the journal tucked underneath his pile of clothes. The guy must have lost it because the entire thing was gibberish. If you want to come down to the station with your ID and some proof that you have a right to his stuff, we'd be more than happy to release it to you. Just stop by when you want to pick it up."

Jamie didn't know what to say, so he thanked Wilks again and showed him out the front door. He walked into the living room, where Sarah was sitting on the couch, eyebrows raised.

"So I take it you heard what he said?" he asked with a smile.

"Why aren't we in the car already? My Jeep is pretty good in the snow," she replied. "We can stop by the hardware store and look for security stuff while we're out."

They headed to the station while Buttons stayed behind to guard the place. Jamie felt slightly guilty about leaving the dog alone in the house since he had no way of saying for sure who'd been inside or whether or not someone was actually following him.

The Jeep handled itself well around the slick corners on the path to the police station. Snowplows were out in force, trying to make sense of the chaos, and they'd made significant progress in clearing off the recent layers of fresh powder. Sarah pulled into the police-station parking lot and scanned for a parking space. The station was a smaller one, and the only visitor spot was full, so they drove around back to find another.

"Why don't you stay here, and I'll run inside to see what I can find?" he suggested, slipping on his gloves.

"If you insist. I guess I'll just have to stay here in the warm and toasty car," she replied.

Jamie rolled his eyes and opened the door. The snow was still coming down in large flakes, and he was covered by the time he walked around the building to the front entrance of the station. Sarah watched with amusement then pulled out her phone and browsed the internet for good security systems. It turned out that searching for the phrase "best security system" returns ads upon ads, so parsing out the signal from the noise was difficult.

Several minutes later, he returned to the car empty-handed. She frowned at him as he opened the door.

"What happened?" she asked.

"The detective isn't back yet, and apparently they're short-staffed today. I'll have to come back," he replied. "Pretty sure the guy at the desk just didn't feel like dealing with me."

The hardware store was completely deserted, aside from the occasional floor associate attempting to look busy. One of the stock boys directed them to the security section, where they picked up a few security cameras and a system they could install themselves.

"There's no way anyone will be able to slip by all of this stuff," Jamie said as he read the back of the camera box.

"You do know how to install this, right?" she asked.

"How hard could it be?"

Installing the system took the latter half of the day and well into the evening. Fortunately, the cameras and sensors all came with adhesive, so they merely had to be stuck on the doors, windows, and walls. That part was so easy a kid could've done it, and that was about the extent of Jamie's home-improvement capabilities.

He sat on the couch, fidgeting with his phone.

"Take a look at this," he said, holding his phone screen out for her to see. "The system can be armed and disarmed directly from my phone. There are sensors on every door and window on the first floor, and there are cameras in the hallways on the first and second floors. I can check the feeds directly from here, and they'll automatically start recording if there's any motion."

"Isn't it kind of creepy to have security cameras inside the house?" she asked.

"You mean creepier than the other stuff in the house? Or how about the stalker that's following us around? I think I can live with a few cameras."

"Fair enough."

No way could anyone enter or leave the house without Jamie knowing. The blaring siren would ensure that.

CHAPTER TWENTY-TWO

THE DESK OFFICER RETURNED FROM the back room with two clear plastic bags and laid them on the counter.

"Sign this please," he said, sliding the clipboard through the slot in the glass.

Jamie scribbled his signature next to the x and slid the form back through the window. The bags were too big to fit through the tray, so the officer opened the door next to the desk and handed the bags to him. One contained a set of clothing and the other a tattered leather-bound book.

He gathered the bags and headed toward the parking lot, where Sarah was waiting in the car. The week had been full of disastrous weather, but it was finally clearing up. The parking lot was paved, and most of the roads were clear. The series of snow days they had been blessed with was coming to an end, so both were preparing to return to campus.

As Jamie walked toward the Jeep, he triumphantly held the bags high in the air and smiled. In the process, he managed to drop a bag in a large puddle, and Sarah laughed as his smile quickly faded.

"You've had them all of five minutes, and you've already managed to destroy evidence. This is why they lock this stuff up." She giggled.

"Very funny. How about you just focus on getting us back to the house safely?" he replied.

"I'll do my best as long as we don't encounter any more puddles along the way."

Buttons yipped from the back seat, not in defense of his owner, but as a reminder that he was still in the car and no one had paid attention to him for several minutes.

"Sorry, buddy." Jamie reached back to give him a pat on the head.

Sarah pulled the Jeep through the wrought iron gate at Turner House and parked in front of the entrance. Jamie climbed the front stairs and opened the door. He was greeted by the electronic beep of the security system and turned toward the security panel to punch in the code. So far, the system had worked flawlessly except for one midnight scare when the dog decided to go for a stroll through the house and tripped the alarm. It scared Buttons more than Jamie, but both were unable to sleep for the rest of the night. He kept the camera feeds on a TV in the bedroom so that he could keep an eye on everything from the bed.

"I'll make some coffee, and you unpack the evidence. Sound good?" she asked.

"Sure. Let's go up to T.J.'s office. It feels like we should examine the evidence where it was found," he replied.

They found nothing special about the clothing, other than it was outdated. T.J. had had the fashion sense of a college professor from the early 1950s. Jamie slid the book out of its plastic bag and onto the mahogany desk. Its binding was marred and tattered by extensive use. The front cover opened with no resistance, as if it had been opened a thousand times before.

```
To J.L.,

My only remaining connection to the
real world. You're more important
than you think. I used what I know
to lead you here, but the rest is
up to you.

Don't use the typewriter until you
understand how it works.

T.J.
```

"J.L. Is that you? I thought you said that you never spent any time with him," Sarah said.

He silently flipped through the next few pages while she waited for a response. After several moments, he turned the book upside down, one hand each on the front and back covers, and shook.

A few scraps of paper fluttered to the ground, as did several photographs that had been wedged between the pages. Some were cracked and yellowed while others were more recent. He sorted through the images on the floor. They found pictures from birthday parties, family vacations, and even a college commencement, and all were of Jamie.

He set the book on the desk and bent down to look at the papers and photos more closely.

Sarah picked up the book and turned through it as Jamie gathered his life into a pile on the floor.

"It's a correspondence journal," she said.

"What's that?" he asked.

"It's a record of all of T.J.'s phone calls and letters, and it looks like all of them were to and from your dad."

As far as Jamie knew, his father had only spoken to T.J. once a year or so, but a dozen pictures must have been there, as well as letters and notes, all scattered on the hardwood. T.J. had collected Jamie's entire life like one of the oddities on his shelves. Most of his major life events were documented in this book as well as some things that even he had forgotten. And then the letters suddenly stopped, two years before, at the same time as his dad's heart.

The journal didn't end with the final letter, though. The remaining pages were filled with writing, in deep black ink. The letters were chaotic, as if written in a panic. Words were scratched out, lines and arrows were scattered on the paper, and that went on for pages and pages.

"What the hell is that?" she asked, holding the book out for him to look.

Jamie examined the writing. Through the chaos, he could see T.J.'s meticulous efforts to craft the perfect sentences, and he recognized the storyline because it was his own.

"It's a first draft," he replied.

"A what?" Sarah was confused.

"It's a first draft. We found the final one in the fireplace."

The pieces of the puzzle slowly came together to form the sickening truth. What Jamie had found in the fireplace was the typed version of the story that was scrawled in the journal. He recognized it only because it was his life. He felt a knot building in his stomach. *It could be some kind of twisted joke, but how? The journal had been locked away since T.J.'s suicide, which occurred well before the events written in it.*

The story itself wasn't written as a journal entry. The scratched-out words and arrows signified that the author had changed bits and pieces of the story. A journal entry should be a retelling of something that already happened, a recounting of facts. This entry was creating something that hadn't happened yet. *But how could that be possible?* It seemed as if T.J. had scripted Jamie's journey, all the way up through his move to the house. The story was skeletal, only recounting the major moments, but everything was there. He had done everything written down here.

Later, Jamie sat on the back patio, running his index finger around the rim of a wine glass and staring off into space. He needed time to think about what was happening, what all of this meant. Something had led him here. It wasn't chance or circumstance. Someone had planned for him to be here. *But why?* T.J.'s scribbles stopped at Jamie's discovery of the contents in the locked drawer, but so much had happened since then. *Was that all scripted too?* He felt truly and utterly powerless, as if he was occupying a world designed for him and controlled by someone else.

"What do you think he meant when he said not to use the typewriter?" Sarah did her best to break the silence because Jamie hadn't said anything for some time.

"It said not to use the typewriter until we know how it works. Maybe it's fragile? I don't know," he replied.

He thought for a second.

"I wonder if T.J. used that typewriter for all of his books. If so, all of this isn't just linked to T.J.— it's linked to that typewriter." He thought back to his first day in the house and to the page that sat in the typewriter carriage. It might have been the last thing that T.J. had ever typed, and it was his attempt at rewriting one of his own stories.

> Annabelle stood on the edge of good
> and evil as a powerful force tugged
> her toward the darkness. She felt
> herself losing control of her hand,
> which threatened to drop the oil
> lamp on the living-room carpet.
> As her hand trembled, she thought
> of her parents, sleeping in their
> bedroom on the second floor. She
> fought to keep control of her arm,
> and just as she started to let go,
> her mother clenched Annabelle's
> hand tightly, preventing the lamp
> from falling to the floor.

A thought had been building in Jamie's mind for some time, but he just couldn't bring himself to say it. It was crazy, and acknowledging it was also an acknowledgment that something truly impossible was happening. None of this was logical. Things such as ghosts weren't real. The past can't be changed. Writing something down doesn't make it real.

"He was trying to change the ending to his first book," he said.

"What are you talking about?" she asked.

"I found that typed page sticking out of the typewriter when Don showed me around the house. It was T.J.'s attempt to rewrite the end to *Satan's Song*. I hadn't read the book at the time, so I didn't recognize it, but it's a revised ending. In the new ending, Annabelle doesn't drop the lantern, and the house doesn't burn down. Everybody lives. Maybe T.J. thought that if he rewrote the ending, he would be able to change what actually happened. He would be able to save the lives of the people who he'd condemned to death with his writing."

"That's insane. Your uncle was insane." The last sentence seemed to slip from Sarah's mouth before she could stop it.

"Then how do you explain all of this? He wrote the books before any of this happened. Unless T.J. actually murdered all of these people and planted all of this stuff so that he could play out some sick fantasy of bringing his books to life, all of this came true on its own."

"The only proof we have is an old wooden box and the journal of a madman," she replied.

"You saw the film just like I did," he said. "You saw whatever it was coming for Louise. You talked to the family. You've seen the death and destruction that these books have caused. It's all linked to that damned typewriter. All of this is linked to it. My story is linked too. That's why T.J. said not to use it."

Jamie wasn't mad at Sarah although he noticed he was raising his voice. He was mad at T.J. for bringing him into all of this, and he wanted out.

"Well, let's just destroy it then," she said sarcastically.

He thought for a second before speaking. "You're onto something now," he said, hopping up from his chair before Sarah could process what was happening.

"I was just kidding. That's not going to help, plus your uncle said not to touch it."

She turned around to face him, but he was already inside. She chased him through the house and up the stairs.

He stood over his uncle's desk, holding a fire poker over his head.

"This is crazy. Stop it!" she pleaded.

The poker came down with one swift blow. It put a small dent in the paper tray but glanced off and nearly hit him in the leg. The typewriter was old and made almost completely out of metal, so Jamie would need more than a fire poker to damage it.

"You're going to hurt yourself." She laughed nervously.

Jamie mulled over his options.

"You're right," he said, lowering the poker.

Sarah's momentary relief was quickly extinguished as Jamie marched over to the window and threw it open.

"What are you doing?" she asked.

"Not hurting myself," he replied as he walked back over to the typewriter.

It was heavy and cumbersome, and the carriage slid back and forth as he carried it across the room and promptly chucked it out the window. It hit the ground with a loud clang. He peered out the window to inspect the damage.

"Now we don't have to worry about it anymore," he said.

She stared at him in disbelief. "You're nuts!" she said, running to the window.

They walked through the house and onto the back porch. The typewriter had landed on the stone pathway behind the house and exploded into several hundred tiny pieces. Type levers and glass keys lay strewn across the grass, and the body of the typewriter was crushed and deformed.

"At least that's that," he said. He left the crumpled mess in the yard and headed back inside.

"Aren't we going to pick it up?" she asked.

"I'll get it tomorrow."

"Are you all right? I've got to run, but I'm a little worried about you. If I come back and there's more stuff out on the lawn, I'm going to start seriously questioning our friendship."

"I'm fine, I promise," he replied.

Later that night, the large canopy bed creaked as Jamie tossed and turned. He played the last few months over in his mind, trying to fabricate a reasonable explanation for everything that had happened. He repeatedly came up empty-handed. Buttons lay at the foot of the bed. He seemed to know his owner was upset and walked to the head of the bed to comfort him.

The typewriter lay splayed across the backyard, and Jamie wondered if he hadn't just destroyed his only chance of solving the ongoing mystery. That had been a gut reaction that he immediately regretted.

CHAPTER
TWENTY-THREE

J AMIE WALKED THE TIGHTROPE BETWEEN the dreaming and the waking world. The furnace rumbled to life, pushing him into reality although reality was more like a dream as of late. He felt the warm blankets touching his skin, and his other senses came into focus. A foul odor slowly crept up thought his nose, and he opened his eyes to be greeted by the dog's gaping mouth. Buttons snored softly, and Jamie got a whiff of kibble with a touch of rotten fish with every breath.

"Come on, man," he said, pushing the dog away from his face. Buttons grunted and repositioned himself on the other side of the bed.

Although the house was warm and cozy, an occasional chill drifted through the air, thanks to the single-pane windows so common in old houses. He slowly rose from the bed and slipped into his house shoes. Buttons stayed behind to steal a few more fleeting minutes of sleep.

The regret from the previous day still hung over him as he walked past T.J.'s open office door toward the staircase. It probably hadn't been the best idea to hurl the machine out the window. He caught something out of the corner of his eye, a subtle flash of black. Jamie backed up until he was parallel with the office door and slowly turned his head. The typewriter was sitting perfectly centered on T.J.'s mahogany desk. After a hard blink, it was still there. He slowly entered the office, peeking in the corners to ensure that no one was waiting for him. The Royal 1 was in pristine condition, with no signs of the poker strike nor the twenty-foot drop from the second-floor window.

I must have dreamt it, but the memories are too vivid. He pulled his phone from his pajama pants, snapped a picture of the typewriter, and sent it to Sarah with the caption *Look what I found this morning.*

He was absolutely positive he had set the house alarm the night before. In fact, it was still armed. He flipped open his laptop lid to check the camera footage from the hallways, but the cameras hadn't been activated all night. If someone had broken in, footage would've been recorded to prove it, but nothing was there.

Jamie let the dog outside and walked to the back of the house, following the stone path to the scene of the typewriter massacre. A hundred or so pieces and fragments had been scattered across the yard the previous night, but all of them were gone now. Nothing was left behind, no evidence of the previous night's chaos. He sat on the back patio, looking at the subdivision below. *Maybe I'm losing grip on reality.* He felt the subtle pulse of his phone in his pocket.

Be right there.

Sarah arrived half an hour later and scoured the surface of the typewriter, looking for any discernible nicks or scratches.

"This can't be the same one," she said. "It's in perfect condition. The other was completely destroyed... This just can't be the same one."

How could a typewriter mysteriously reassemble itself after a fall from two stories, and who had put it back in the house?

"We have to try it again," she said.

"Try what?" he replied.

"Throw it out the window. We'll see if it happens again. Only... let me do it this time. You can't have all the fun."

They went upstairs, and he opened the window for her and waved her on. She had a much harder time picking the typewriter up than he did, but she managed. She set it on the window ledge and launched it over with as much force as she could muster. The machine once again plummeted toward the stone path below. This time, they both watched as it exploded on impact.

"Now get the key to the object cases. We'll lock it up in there and check on it tomorrow. There's no way anyone's going to break that open."

They had a terrible time collecting all the typewriter pieces from the yard, and gathering everything and lugging the pieces up the stairs took nearly an hour. Jamie tucked everything neatly under the third empty case and locked it shut. They both stood back.

"You can't fit a house under there," he said.

She gave him a puzzled look. "Right..."

"Rumor had it that Turner House was the topic of the third book in the trilogy, right? I hadn't thought about it before, but T.J. chose three cases for his objects. Why would he have a third if the book was going to be about the house? A house wouldn't fit under one of these little cases."

"But the typewriter fits perfectly," Sarah added.

"Could this be the third object?" he asked.

She didn't say anything but looked over at Jamie, who met her gaze.

Jamie pulled one of the web cameras down from the hallway and moved it into T.J.'s office with both the object case and the mahogany desk in frame. He connected the webcam to an external hard drive so that he would be able to record everything that happened in the room. This time, he was determined to catch something.

The living-room table became their mobile command center. He set the camera feed to display on the TV while she searched the web and tried to find anything she could on the typewriter. They agreed to take shifts, to make sure somebody kept an eye on the feed at all times.

The dog's whine woke Jamie, who was asleep on the couch. He had failed to honor his shift as security guard. Fortunately, the broken typewriter remained locked away under the domed glass, still in pieces. Sarah was leaning up against him, surrounded by a cocoon of blankets. She must have fallen over as she dozed. He didn't move right away and sat there savoring the moment before another whine reminded him of the task at hand.

Buttons was standing on his hind legs at the back door, preemptively eyeing a fresh spot to relieve himself. He hadn't had an accident in the house since he was a pup, but the clock was ticking. Jamie made it to the door just as the dog started to panic, and he bolted outside as soon as he had enough clearance.

Jamie stepped outside to watch Buttons bounce around in the backyard and soak in the crisp winter air. The last few days had been warm, and most of the snow had melted, but the cold night air had left everything covered in a fresh layer of frost. Once the dog was finished, he locked the door behind himself and walked back into the living room. Jamie reclaimed his spot, slipping back into the small groove between Sarah and the arm of the couch. He glanced up at the screen, and what he saw caused him to jump to his feet, nearly knocking Sarah onto the floor.

"What, what's going on?" she asked, emerging from a sleepy haze.

"Look at the feed," he said, pointing at the television screen.

The glass display case was empty, and the typewriter sat in pristine condition on T.J.'s grand writing desk.

"Do you have the key?" she asked.

"It's been in my pocket this whole time," he replied. He patted his pants pocket to confirm.

They ran upstairs to T.J.'s office. Sarah walked over to the empty case and pulled on the wooden frame. It didn't budge.

"Still locked," she said.

"Let's check the feed." As they sat in front of his laptop, Jamie scrubbed back and forth through the recorded video file. "Here!"

The typewriter sat in pieces under the glass dome. As the video progressed, static formed over the pile. At the same time, the same haze appeared at the center of the mahogany desk. As the broken bits faded into nothingness, the restored typewriter appeared on the desk. The event took only five seconds or so and must have happened while he was outside with the dog.

"Guess we don't have to worry about anyone breaking into the house anymore," she said.

"I think I'd prefer a burglar at this point," he replied, still scrubbing back and forth on the video and unable to believe what he was seeing. In mere seconds, the broken machine was able to repair itself and teleport to the desk. It wasn't someone hiding in the house or a practical joke—this was something neither Sarah nor Jamie could explain.

"What do we do now?" she asked.

"We type something," he replied without hesitation.

The Royal Standard 1 was, as the name implied, the first Royal typewriter. It had been produced in the early 1900s and was a glorious flop. At the time, it was considered a portable typewriter, but that was hard to believe due to its weight. Sarah had spent some time researching T.J.'s typewriter, which was relatively easy to identify, given the large "1" on either side of the front body and the words "Royal Standard" on the paper tray. She even did a web search for its serial number although she'd found no matches.

They stood in front of the typewriter, unsure of what to do next.

"This doesn't seem like a good idea," she said. She recalled T.J.'s note inside the journal, warning Jamie not to use the typewriter until he knew how it worked. Neither of them knew how it worked, but they now knew it was the cause of all of the tragedy surrounding T.J.'s stories. They also knew he had tried to rewrite the end of one of them with no luck. Clearly, Emily, the real Annabelle, had still perished regardless of the new ending. The reason why T.J.'s experiment had failed was unclear. Whatever that was, it had been enough to drive the author to suicide, and that was causing her to pause.

"We have to try. How else are we going to figure out how it works? We typed on it before, remember? It should be fine as long as we stick with simple, innocuous things," he said.

"I don't know. Isn't there someone else who might know more about stuff like this before we go typing out our fates?"

"There's only one other person who knows about the books," Jamie said.

She looked over at him and groaned. "Are you sure that it's a good idea to bring him back into this?" she asked.

"He might know something about this sort of thing. He figured out the connection between T.J.'s book and the family in New Haven, so maybe he could help with this," he replied. "I'll give him a call."

CHAPTER TWENTY-FOUR

J AMIE LED SEBASTIAN THROUGH THE front door and into the entryway. The man stood in awe as the massive house appeared to overwhelm his senses. "I've dreamt of this place," he said, "but it's even more fantastic than I had imagined."

He peered into a miniature curiosity cabinet hanging from a wall, examining a small piece of coral sitting inside. As he walked down the hallway, he traced his finger along a wooden shelf of specimen jars.

"These are pretty hard to get," he said. "Some of them might even be illegal to possess."

Jamie was neither surprised that Sebastian could identify what was in the jars from sight nor that possession of some of his uncle's things was prohibited by law. He had taken a risk in bringing the man to Turner House but hoped the oddity collector could provide some insight into the mysterious abilities of the typewriter. He glanced at Sarah out of the corner of his eye, and she was wearing a deep scowl. She had pleaded with him not to bring Sebastian. In fact, she threatened to stay home with the cat, but Jamie begged her to come, which she reminded him of several times throughout the visit.

"The typewriter is upstairs in T.J.'s office," Jamie said, gesturing toward the staircase.

Sebastian waddled up the stairs like a toddler who was doing it for the first time. He wasn't very old, by any stretch of the imagination, but his knees seemed fused in position and unable to bend.

The typewriter sat in pristine condition despite two trips out the window and a blow from a fire poker.

"I can't believe that I'm standing in T.J. Lawson's office," Sebastian said. "This is incredible." He stepped over to the typewriter on the writing desk, and his eyes widened as he brushed his fingers over the keys. "Do you know when he got it?"

"No idea," Jamie replied. "We figure that it must have been sometime around the late eighties, prior to writing his first book."

Sebastian examined it carefully, pressing his bulbous nose up against the keys to get a better look inside. Nothing was physically unique about the typewriter. It was old, of course, but it had no unordinary markings or unique characteristics that gave any indication of its history.

"Have you ever heard of anything like this before?" Jamie asked. He hoped the man's expertise in the occult would provide some answers.

"There are a few distinct possibilities," Sebastian replied.

Jamie found his confidence reassuring.

"Both of them involve a connection to another world, lightning rods if you will. In the late eighteen hundreds, spiritualists started to use a process called automatic writing to channel supernatural sources. They would act as a conduit for these sources and allow them to send messages through their hands and onto paper. Sometimes, the writings were gibberish, but other times they contained important messages from the spirit world. It's possible that your uncle was receiving messages of the future from some sort of spiritual power. Of course, this means that the connection would have died with your uncle and has nothing to do with the typewriter. The only way to tell if this is the case is to try it for ourselves."

Jamie looked over at Sarah and cocked his head as if to say "I told you so."

"But no one has ever proven that any of those things are real," Sarah retorted. "Haven't you heard of James Randi? For decades, he offered people a million dollars to prove that they had psychic abilities, but no one was ever able to claim the prize."

"I'm just telling you what I know. You did ask me here for my expertise, correct?" He shot Sarah a cold glance. "Let's start with something simple."

Sebastian rolled a blank sheet of paper into the carriage of the typewriter and thought for a minute.

"Stand on the other side of the room," he said to Sarah. "I don't want you to see what I'm typing."

"All right," she said, less than enthused. She stepped to the other side of the room, next to the object cases.

Sebastian typed something.

Sarah held up three fingers, then five, then none.

"Sarah," he said. "Pick three numbers."

She held out her right hand with three fingers in the air. Jamie felt the hairs on the back of his neck stand up.

"Okay," he said.

She held up all five fingers, then she clenched her fist and made a zero.

"Why didn't you just say them out loud?" Sebastian asked, looking back and forth between her hands and what he had typed on the page.

"I don't know. I didn't really think about it," she replied.

"Come over here and look at this," he said.

Sarah stepped over and looked at the single typed line. She said nothing but backed away slowly. The color drained from her face.

"I didn't say, 'Choose a number from zero to five.' You could have picked any number, yet you chose these three," he said. "Now you try something," he said to Jamie.

Jamie pulled the carriage return and started to type another line.

```
It rained
```

They waited for several moments, but nothing happened.

"Try being more specific," Sebastian said.

Jamie added to the line.

```
It rained at Turner House at 11:07
a.m. on February 20th, 2019.
```

The time was 11:06, and Jamie, Sarah, and Sebastian stood in silence for one of the longest minutes of their lives. The sky was sunny outside with no prediction of rain.

11:07.

Sebastian walked to the window and peered outside.

"Not a dro—"

He was cut off by the sound of droplets hitting the roof. First came a drizzle, followed by a downpour.

Sarah said what the others already knew. "Whatever we type comes true."

T.J. hadn't been a conduit, and no spirits had been whispering the future. The typewriter determined the future.

"You could type anything," Sebastian said, wrestling with the meaning of his own statement. "Anything."

"We should try something else," she said.

"Like a winning lottery ticket," Sebastian said.

"No. We can't just go typing whatever we want. We have no idea how this affects the rest of the world. What if making it rain here causes a drought somewhere else? T.J. wrote a few stories that somehow glommed onto the lives of real people. It ruined lives. It killed people," he said.

Jamie thought back to T.J.'s note.

> I'm surrounded by the death and
> destruction that I've created, and
> there's nothing that I can do to
> fix it.

"He must have figured some of this out," Jamie said. "He even tried to rewrite the ending, but it didn't stick for some reason. He killed himself because he couldn't fix the damage that he'd caused, but he sure as hell tried. There must be some reason why he couldn't save his characters, and we shouldn't use this until we truly understand how it works."

Sebastian stepped forward and put his hand over the keys. Jamie started to intervene but stood back instead. The metal letters thwacked against the carriage.

> T.J. Lawson never published Satan's
> Song.

"Have your copy of the book?" Sebastian asked.

Sarah ran downstairs to grab her copy of T.J.'s first novel and returned a few minutes later. "Still here," she said.

"So, there's your answer," he replied. "You can't rewrite the past. Once it's done, it's done. That's simple enough."

"T.J. even said it in his suicide note," Jamie said. He seemed to be mulling something over. "But if T.J. knew that he couldn't fix any of this, then why would he bring me here?"

"That's a good question. You know, you should let me take this back to the shop and have a closer look," Sebastian said, as if he had wanted to say it for some time and it finally burst out of him. "I know a few folks who might be able to help us figure out how it actually works."

Jamie sensed an air of desperation in his voice. Letting the man walk away with a device that could gift its owner with anything the heart desired seemed like a bad idea.

Sarah said what Jamie had been thinking. "I think that we should keep it here."

Jamie caught a glimmer of contempt in Sebastian's eyes before they darted to him for confirmation.

"She's right," Jamie said. "We better leave it here for now, but let us know what you find, and try to keep this whole thing under wraps."

"I'll see what I can do," Sebastian said, barely able to hide his disappointment. "I better get going pretty soon. How about that tour that you promised? I would love to see the place."

Jamie walked Sebastian around the second floor. As he wrapped up on the second floor and descended the staircase, he heard a yip from below. Jamie had been so preoccupied with the events of the day that he had forgotten Buttons was outside in the rain. He hurried to kitchen to rescue the dog, who was standing up on his hind legs, peering into the kitchen window. He was soaked and shivering.

"I'm so sorry, bud," he said as he grabbed a towel from the cupboard. He wrapped the towel around the dog's torso and vigorously dried him off.

Sebastian returned from exploring the first floor sitting room and walked toward Buttons. "Poor guy," he said as he reached to pat him on the head.

Buttons lifted his head and snarled, the growl coming from deep inside. This startled Sebastian, who pulled his hand back and stepped backward.

"Hey!" Jamie swatted the dog on the nose with his finger. "I'm sorry," he said. "He's never like this. He must be freaked out from standing in the rain."

"It's no problem," Sebastian replied, maintaining his distance.

Jamie finished drying Buttons off and sent him upstairs with Sarah. He showed Sebastian around the rest of the house and then walked him out to his car. The rain had stopped by then, and the sun was shining brightly through the trees.

"Thanks for helping us out," he said, offering his hand to Sebastian.

"It's not a problem. I hope you'll keep me in mind if you ever decide to depart with anything in your uncle's collection. I'd love to add some of this to the exhibit. And I really think you should let me take the typewriter with me," he said, eyes darting toward the ground. "I could help more if you just let me take it."

"I think that it's best that it stays with us for now. I promise we'll keep you updated," Jamie said, as nicely as he could.

Sebastian climbed into his old rusted van, which took quite a bit of effort, considering his short stature. The door creaked shut, and he waved as he pulled away in a cloud of burning oil smoke. Jamie felt bad for the guy. He had nothing in the world except for an old van and a collection of fake mermaids and yard-sale junk. He doubted that Sebastian had any ill intentions and chalked his weird behavior up to poor social skills. Either way, he was the only person Jamie knew of who would be knowledgeable enough to help or at least take the story seriously.

Jamie walked back to the house and into the kitchen, where Sarah sat waiting with a cup of coffee.

"Get rid of him?"

"Yep, he left a few minutes ago," he replied.

"I don't think that we should have brought him into this. Did you see the look that he gave me when I said that we should leave the typewriter here? There's something off about him."

"I know, I know. But he might be the only person who can help us. He's just a weird dude—that's all. There's nothing wrong with that," he replied. "Let's see what he comes up with, and then we can decide if we want to work with him or not."

Jamie felt as if the fate of the world was in his hands, at least the fates of Louise McAulle, Emily, and Emily's family. So many lives had been changed by the *Dreadful Objects*, and the typewriter was behind it all. He wasn't sure he would be able to bring anyone back, but he had to try, and he had to try very carefully.

T.J. must have discovered the truth about his writing shortly after the events of *Cellulose* unfolded before him. If Louise was his inspiration for the book, he was likely devastated by her death. They still weren't sure how he had connected everything to the typewriter, but he had attempted to right his wrongs and rewrite the end of *Satan's Song*. That was the last thing he'd ever written, and Jamie found the evidence sitting in the typewriter on his first day inside the house.

The two sat at the kitchen table for some time with Buttons curled up under their feet. They talked about the day's events and tried to make sense out of everything that had happened. Neither could quite comprehend the power of the device sitting in the room upstairs. They wanted to test it further and figure out the rules by which it played, but fear of irreversible damage kept them from action. The last person who had tried to use it ended up with a gun in his mouth.

CHAPTER TWENTY-FIVE

"SO, HE BANGS HIS FISTS on the table in the meeting, stands up and points at the director, and says, 'I won't let you singlehandedly destroy this department!' Then he storms out, and the room is completely silent. You could have heard a pin drop." Sarah paused her story to take a drink of wine.

"You're kidding. And this is normal?" Jamie asked.

"Maybe not quite normal, but there's usually shouting of some sort at most faculty meetings. We're going through the budgeting process for the upcoming year, and things are pretty tense."

"Ours were never that bad back in Pittsburgh," he replied.

They stood at a small bar table, in the middle of a busy wine shop. The owner held tastings on Fridays and Saturdays, and the place was always packed. Both Sarah and Jamie were happy for the momentary reprieve from the events of the past few days, and this night felt a little different than the others they had spent together. It was definitely a date, or at least it felt that way. He'd made it a point to formally ask her to dinner and a movie and hoped she got the hint. The night still felt somewhat strange to him, as if he was treading in forbidden territory, but the feelings of guilt had started to subside.

After the wine tasting, they walked across the street to the movie theater to catch a late screening of a new thriller. Jamie felt warm and fuzzy from the wine. Not to be deterred by the large amount of cheese consumed at the wine shop, or the dinner earlier, he bought the largest size of popcorn available.

"Are you going to eat all of that?" she asked.

"No, but we are," he replied.

They settled into their seats and talked over the commercials. As the lights dimmed, so did the outside world.

They sat in the darkness, and Jamie slowly started to inch his hand toward Sarah's on the armrest. Something, maybe the wine, had cracked his outer shell.

Just as he had nearly finished the journey to the armrest, Jamie's phone vibrated against his seat, resulting in a loud buzz that made them both jump. He picked it up and checked the screen. Sarah must have noticed the scowl on his face.

"What is it?" she whispered.

"Someone just opened the front door, and the alarm's going off," he replied as he rose from his seat, jolted out of his wine-induced bliss.

"Oh my God," she said. "Let's go."

Jamie left his mammoth popcorn behind, and they both ran from the theater and back to the car. The Subaru's tires squealed against the wet concrete as he pulled out of the parking lot. In only a few minutes, they made it back to the house, a few blocks away.

The police hadn't gotten there yet, and the gate was still wide open.

"Why didn't I lock the gate? I'm so stupid!" he said while pulling the car up to the front entryway. "Stay here and lock the doors."

"Just wait for the police." Sarah was panicking, worried about whatever might be waiting for him inside the house.

Jamie had already climbed out of the car, though. He started to walk up the front stairs and turned back toward her. "I'll be fine!" he yelled back at her. "Just lock the door and stay put. If anything happens, get out of here."

She rolled up the driver's side window, moved over to the driver's seat, and hit the door lock.

Something was off. Jamie walked up the front steps and could see the door was slightly ajar. No glass was broken, though. A sickening thought washed over him. He sprinted up the staircase and into T.J.'s office. The grand desk was bare, and the typewriter was nowhere to be found. He still had the camera set up in the office and ran to his laptop downstairs to check the feed. He scrubbed through the video, just in time to see what had caused the alarm, before the police arrived.

Jamie heard the police sirens approaching the house and slammed the laptop shut. As he walked out the front door, he was met with flashlights and drawn guns.

"Stop and put your hands in front of you!" the officer shouted.

"It's okay. It's okay. It was a false alarm," he replied, complying with the officer and holding his hands out.

"Wait!" Sarah exclaimed as she opened the car door.

"Ma'am, stay in the car." The officer held a palm out.

She complied. "He owns the house," she added in a panic.

The officers approached Jamie and asked for identification. He pulled his wallet from his back pocket and handed it to one of the men. The officer returned to his patrol car to run the ID through the computer. After a few tense moments, he returned with the wallet.

"Everything checks out. Are you sure that you don't want us to take a look?" he asked.

"It's really okay. I tripped it when I opened the front door and didn't get the code into the panel fast enough. Sorry to waste your time," he replied.

The officers headed back to their squad cars and pulled away.

"Thank God it was a false alarm," she said, hugging him tightly.

"It wasn't. You have to help me find the dog," he replied.

"What the hell are you talking—"

"Just help me find Buttons!" He raised his voice this time.

They both shouted for the dog as they walked through the house. When Jamie heard a whimper coming from the hall closet, he ran to the door and turned the knob. Buttons bolted through the door to him, crying with excitement.

"Bud, are you okay?" he asked, almost expecting an answer.

The dog was a little rattled but showed no signs of injury.

"Someone locked him in there? What's going on?" Sarah was confused and losing her patience.

Jamie grabbed her by the hand and led her into the living room. He opened the laptop to the video file. Although he had moved the first-floor camera to T.J.'s office, another camera was still in the second-floor hallway. A portly figure emerged from the staircase, and they watched as Sebastian walked across the hallway to T.J.'s office. Jamie switched to the office feed just in time to see Sebastian struggling to lift the typewriter. He left the room and went down the stairs, out of the frame. That must have alerted Buttons, who appeared in the bedroom doorway and followed him down the staircase.

"He must have been hiding somewhere, waiting for us to leave." Jamie walked to check the back door. "There's no broken glass at the front or back doors."

Sarah shivered at the idea of a man hiding in the house, watching their every move.

Jamie walked the first floor to look for any weaknesses in the perimeter. The window in the back sitting room was ajar. Sebastian must have opened it during the house tour when Jamie was distracted with the dog. The thought of the man trying to climb through the back window was comical, but he'd managed to do it somehow. Clearly, he had planned to steal the typewriter all along. Jamie didn't know what Sebastian was going to do with it but could only hope he'd wait a day or two before using it. *That would give me enough time to get it back.*

"Why the hell did you tell them that it was a false alarm?" Sarah asked, standing behind him.

"Well, officer, someone stole our magic typewriter, and we'd really like it back," Jamie said sarcastically. He quickly realized he was being a jackass and softened his tone. "I'm sorry. I mean we don't want to scare him off with the police. Plus, it's not like he can damage it. We can go back to New Haven and get it from him ourselves."

"What? We've got to contact the police. The guy's probably nuts. What if he's dangerous or figures out we're coming after him and uses the typewriter against us? 'Jamie and Sarah died in a fire' would take him all of five seconds to type." Sarah was clearly irritated by Jamie's cavalier attitude.

"And this whole thing isn't nuts already? We can't tell the police. If he wanted to kill us, he could have typed it up before he walked away with the typewriter. I don't think he's dangerous. The cameras were fairly hidden, so he may not even know that we suspect him."

"What are you talking about? The typewriter happens to be stolen shortly after he comes for a visit, and you think he won't expect us to come after him? Of course he expects us. We can't do this. Someone's going to get hurt," she said.

"We can figure this out. We're close, and I can feel it. If we get it back, we may still be able to save the characters in T.J.'s books. Go with me. We'll get some sleep and head up there tomorrow morning. Please."

"And what makes you think that you can save them? T.J. proved that he couldn't change the past. He tried with Emily and failed. This isn't your burden. He's the one that killed all of those people, not you. All that you're going to do is end up getting hurt or worse." Her voice had started to crack. "You'll just be another one of his victims."

"I'm not a victim. Why are you getting so upset about this?" Jamie was caught off guard by her sudden show of emotion.

"Because I care about you," she blurted out. "I more than care about you."

"What do you mean?" he asked. Something else had obviously been on her mind.

"Don't you get it? Don't you feel it at all when we spend time together? Look, I know that what you went through is terrible, and you've had to deal with a lot of grief, so I haven't pushed it, but isn't there a part of you that wonders about us? Or is this really all just about the typewriter?"

He didn't know what to say, so he said nothing.

"I guess that answers the question," she said, turning to leave.

Jamie's feet were glued to the floor. He hadn't expected the conversation to go there and didn't know how to deal with it. So he didn't. He heard Sarah's footsteps cross the hardwood. She opened the door and slammed it shut behind herself.

CHAPTER TWENTY-SIX

"YOU'LL HAVE FUN HERE, BUD," Jamie said as he handed Buttons' leash over to the dreadlocked owner of the doggy day care. The pup was clearly unhappy, and Jamie knew why. He'd never seen this man before, and the place must have been covered with the scent of dozens of other dogs.

"We'll take good care of you," the man said, tossing him a meat-flavored treat.

It bounced off of his nose and onto the floor. Buttons must have gotten just enough of a whiff to pique his interest. He picked the treat up and chomped.

Jamie walked out to the car and climbed into the driver's seat. He was alone again but knew bringing the dog along for the ride would be irresponsible this time. He had no idea how many days he would be in New Haven or what he would find when he got there. The only thing he knew was that he wasn't coming back without the typewriter. He hoped he wouldn't lose Sarah in the process.

The cheery weather contrasted with Jamie's inner turmoil. His eyes followed the horizon, but his mind was elsewhere. His playlist had stopped twenty minutes before, but he hadn't noticed. After several voice mails and texts, Jamie had gone directly to Sarah's apartment and rung the buzzer. He could see her car in the parking lot, but she'd refused to come to the door.

He felt terrible about how he'd left things with her but knew he still had to go to New Haven. Once he was able to reclaim the typewriter, he might actually be able to get to the bottom of what was happening. He might be able to fix things, to undo all the terrible things his uncle's stories had created. He wasn't sure how, but he had to try. Still, Jamie couldn't shake a feeling telling him to turn around and forget all about the typewriter and Sebastian. It told him to speed back to Sarah, apologize, and move on with his life while he had the chance. He hadn't been prepared for what she'd said the night before, but if he had another chance, he would tell her he felt the same way.

Something was different about Sebastian's World of Intrigue. As he drove by the building, Jamie noticed that no parking spaces were available along the road. The side streets were packed too. The garish neon signs were obscured by a line of people, which extended down the street and around the block. *That bastard had the nerve to put the typewriter on display.* The possessed typewriter of a famous horror novelist would make a great attraction. Jamie had planned to confront the man in an empty storefront, take the typewriter back, and be on his way. The guy wasn't exactly a prime human specimen, so the physical threat was minimal, but the crowd would make things significantly more complicated. *How could I have thought that I'd simply waltz right in and take it?*

Jamie sat across the street for a few minutes, looking for any sign of Sebastian, but he couldn't see the round little thief anywhere. He knew he had to figure out a way to distract the crowd, get in, take the typewriter back, and escape without detection. *But how?* After a few laps around the block to develop a plan, he came up with nothing. Jamie parked the car a few blocks down from the World of Intrigue in front of a small coffee shop and hoped a bit of caffeine would bring some inspiration.

The café was overwhelmed with customers. The teenager behind the counter was taking orders and shouting them to the elderly barista, who appeared to be hard of hearing. Despite the hearing impediment, the way she glided through the kitchen made it clear that she'd worked in the coffee shop for years. She effortlessly went from making drinks to making sandwiches, all while keeping the impatient caffeine addicts appeased with a set of rapid-fire jokes.

Getting his order took several minutes, then Jamie found a seat at a small corner table. He was used to the background hum of a coffee shop, but this place had more of a dull roar.

"Mind if I sit?"

He looked up, and Sarah was standing over him.

"What are you doing here? I thought you didn't want to come." A sense of relief washed over him. For a moment, he forgot all about the task at hand and was just happy to have her back.

"I couldn't let you do this by yourself. I'd feel terrible if something happened. You came by the apartment, and I felt so guilty after you left that I decided to come. And I'm glad that I did, because you could really do a better job with the whole incognito thing. I saw you sitting across the street from Sebastian's."

"You followed me all the way here? Why didn't you just call? We could have at least ridden together," he said.

"I don't know. I wasn't sure how things would go, given our conversation yesterday. Clearly, this is important to you, and I was afraid you might back out if I offered to come. I also thought it might have been awkward."

"Awkward? I feel like an ass for what happened yesterday. I should have told you how I felt, and I froze. I should have told you how much I care about you. I do wonder what it would be like if we actually tried to date. At first, I felt so guilty for even thinking it, but I'm the one that's putting all the guilt on myself. Lilly would have been the first to say that I should do whatever makes me happy. And you make me happy."

Sarah smiled. "I'm glad to hear that. What are we going to do about Sebastian, though? His place is packed."

"I don't know. We can't just stroll in. I wish that we had some way to clear the place out," he replied.

Jamie wasn't prepared to be arrested for breaking and entering at night, but he knew that only so much sneaking could be done amid a large crowd of people while the place was open.

"We could just set the building on fire. That would do it," Sarah said dryly. She was joking, of course.

"Maybe something a little less murdery," he replied.

She thought for a moment then giggled. "Stink bombs, then. You know, those little glass capsules that you smash on the ground. Kids used to bring them on the school bus when I was little and break them on the floor. We could break some inside and wait for the place to clear out."

That was a bit juvenile, he thought, but it just might work.

"I don't suppose you have any with you?" he asked with a smirk.

Sarah reached into her purse and withdrew her closed hand. "No, of course I don't have any," she said, opening her empty palm and shoving it into Jamie's face. She pulled out her phone and did a quick web search.

"Well, we could make them. All we'd have to do is put some match sticks in ammonia," she said.

"That's pretty easy," he replied.

"Oh, never mind. It takes a week. I'm guessing that we don't have that long. It looks like there's a magic-and-joke shop thirty minutes north. I'm sure we could find some there."

"Let's go, then!" he said.

They left the café, climbed into Jamie's car, and pulled away.

Barry's Magic and More sat in the middle of a rundown strip mall. The storefront was pristine and somewhat out of place, considering its disheveled surroundings. It appeared to be the only open business in the mall, and the parking lot was completely empty except for a van, which Jamie assumed belonged to the owner of the shop.

The walls of the store were lined with various gags like trick gum packs and whoopee cushions. A row of novelty masks sat on a shelf high above the glass display counter.

A man, presumably Barry, sat behind the counter on a stool, reading a newspaper. He hopped up at the sight of his guests.

"What can I do for you today?" he asked, almost too eager to please.

"We're looking for stink bombs," Jamie replied.

"Well, you've come to the right place. We have three different kinds, Putrid Pods, Silent but Deadly Devils, and good ol' fashion stink bombs."

"Whichever one smells the worst," Sarah replied.

"Devils it is. Gotta keep these locked up. Kids used to steal 'em all the time," Barry said as he unlocked the glass display case. He took his seat on the stool in front of the counter and slid his glasses to the tip of his nose so that he could read the price tag. Then he punched the numbers into the cash register. "Anything else for you today?"

"That should do it," Jamie replied.

"There's three in here. Just toss one on the ground to break the capsule, and it will clear a whole room," he said.

"What about that set of walkie-talkies?" Sarah asked, pointing to the pair in the display case.

"Oh, those aren't actually walkie-talkies," the store owner said. "They're flasks. No, if you want real walkie-talkies, there's an electronics store down the road."

Jamie gave Sarah a puzzled glance.

"What? I thought that they might come in handy," she replied.

He slid the money over the counter and took the paper bag of stink bombs. They returned to the car and drove back toward Sebastian's after a quick stop for a pair of walkie-talkies.

The plan was simple. Sarah would call Sebastian's number and keep him busy while Jamie sneaked into the building, dropped one or two of the newly acquired stink bombs, then waited for the place to clear out. The building was small and not well ventilated, so a well-placed stink bomb should do a sufficient amount of damage.

She made the call, and he approached the storefront. The line still extended around the block.

Jamie skipped the line and went straight for the door to peer inside. Sebastian was standing at the front counter with his back toward him, and a small pimple-faced kid was taking tickets at the entrance to the exhibit. Jamie squeezed his way through the door into the gift shop and looked for a place to deliver the payload. A small fan sat in the corner of the room, and he knew he'd found the perfect place. He slid along the wall, navigating through the crowd, and discreetly dropped the capsule in front of the fan. It didn't break on impact, but he rectified that with the heel of his shoe. Jamie quickly made his escape before the ammonium sulfide started to do its dirty work. The scent of rotten eggs filled his nose as he exited the building, and it smelled exactly like the stuff gas companies put into natural gas to warn of gas leaks.

The smell quickly permeated the room then the entire building. This sent the exhibit goers into a panic, and they quickly poured out the front and back doors of the building. Jamie waited around the back of the building, next to the exit door leading into the exhibit room. Although it was locked from the outside, only a few seconds passed before someone inside pushed it open to escape. He held the door open for the evacuees and waited for Sarah to give the all clear. She watched the commotion from a safe distance across the street and saw Sebastian waddle out of the front doorway, red-faced and angry.

"He's coming out of the front," she said over the walkie.

Jamie slipped through the back door and into the back entryway. A set of stairs rose to his left, which must have led to Sebastian's apartment. The doorway in front of him led to the back of the exhibit, and he stepped through it to begin the search for the typewriter. The place smelled terrible, and he had to hold his breath to keep from gagging. Everything looked exactly as it had during his last visit. He scoured the exhibit room, but no typewriter was in sight. That's when it hit him. He glanced over to the bookcase concealing Sebastian's secret room.

The shelves blocking the door desperately needed grease, and Jamie did his best to slide them out of the way as quietly as possible. All that stood between him and the typewriter was the heavy wooden door, or so he thought. He turned the handle, but the door wouldn't budge. *It's locked.*

"He just turned and went back inside," Sarah said over the walkie.

Jamie had little time to think. He quickly slid the shelves back into place. He could hear Sebastian's footsteps in the front room, so he tiptoed over to the back door and slipped outside. As he did, he pulled out the crumpled-up receipt from the joke shop and wedged it between the doorframe and the latch mechanism. This would ensure easy entry later. A small alleyway led to the business on the other side of the block. He called for Sarah over the walkie-talkie, and she pulled into the business parking lot and picked him up.

"No luck?" she asked.

"I think he's keeping it in that back room behind the bookcase, but it was locked," he replied.

"Why the line of people then, if the typewriter wasn't even on display?" she asked.

"He must have used it. How else could he have become so popular overnight?"

"So what do we do now? How are you going to get back in?" she asked.

"We'll have to come back tonight," he said. "I stuck something in the back door, so hopefully I can slip right in."

The thought of sneaking in made him anxious, but Jamie knew that was the only option.

CHAPTER
TWENTY-SEVEN

EVERY HOTEL ROOM IN NEW Haven was completely booked. Jamie went from place to place but received the same story. People had come from all over to visit Sebastian's crummy little tourist trap. He finally found a vacant room at a motel on the outskirts of town. It looked like a place that was rentable by the hour, and he was pretty sure the office manager might have been a murderous madman in disguise, à la *Psycho*. Either way, it was the only place in the area with a vacant room. Jamie walked out of the office and gave a thumbs-up to Sarah, who was sitting in her car, which they had gone back to pick up after the excursion to the magic shop. He didn't like the look of the place at all, but she was happy to have somewhere to rest her head for a bit.

Wiggling the key into the door lock to the motel room took some force. The place had no fancy keycards, just an old-fashioned room key attached to a long wooden key chain with the room number written in permanent marker. It reminded Jamie of the bathroom hall passes from high school. The haze hovering over the room's dated furniture was caused by a sliver of fluorescent light outside that sneaked through the curtains and refracted through the dust motes. A single queen bed sat in the middle of the room. He hoped Sarah wouldn't mind, but the room was the only one left. Jamie set his duffel bag in the chair since the floor was covered with mysterious stains.

Sarah gingerly rolled back the sheets, trying not to touch the comforter that had been slept in a thousand times before.

"I'll take the couch," Jamie said.

"Don't be silly. That thing is gross. We can share," she replied.

He lay down next to her, and she flipped on the tiny television sitting on top of the dresser, hoping to distract them from the task ahead and the filth surrounding them. The local channels were all news, but she managed to find a station playing old reruns of a cheesy sitcom. It reminded Jamie of weeknights growing up. He would rush home from school to spend time with his dad before he went off to work at night. This usually included a sitcom or two. He and Sarah talked for a while about their childhoods and high school. Although over a decade had passed since graduation, the memories were still strangely vivid. Sarah's mom had divorced her dad during senior year, so it put a damper on what should have been a very exciting time in her life. Her mom eventually remarried, but the new husband was, in Sarah's opinion, an ass. The recent argument with her mom had stemmed from comments she'd made about Sarah's lifestyle and the fact that she was nearly thirty and still unmarried without children. Her mom had never criticized her before the new marriage, and Sarah knew she was being fed lines by her second husband.

Eventually, Sarah nodded off, and Jamie set his phone alarm for early in the morning. He lay in the bed for several hours while thoughts swirled around in his head. When sleep finally came, it was full of paranoid dreams.

Jamie woke up several minutes before the alarm would sound. Sarah had rolled over and put an arm around him in her sleep. He debated whether or not to wake her and lay there for a moment with his hand wrapped around her arm. Eventually, he gently squeezed her arm to wake her.

"What's wrong?" she asked, still half asleep.

"It's almost two, so we should probably get moving," he replied.

Jamie would have to slip in through the back door, break into Sebastian's secret room, grab the typewriter, and slip out, all without detection. The plan could fail in many ways, so Sarah would stay outside in the car and serve as a lookout. Retrieving the typewriter wasn't worth both of them being arrested, so the plan was for her to bail if things went downhill.

Jamie had bought an all-black ensemble and a small crowbar before they arrived at the motel. He was hoping he might be able to jimmy the door latch to the typewriter room with a credit card. Although he'd never used a credit card to unlock a door before, the concept was relatively straightforward, but the crowbar would serve as a backup plan.

The buildings on Sebastian's street were dark, aside from a dive bar down the road. The lights on the first and second floor of the World of Intrigue were off, which meant Sebastian was likely fast asleep, wiped out from the success from the day's visitors, ideally. Jamie parked his car down the street from his building.

"Okay. Stay here, and I'll call with the walkie if I need any help. You be on the lookout for any lights on the second floor. If you see any, tap the call button on the walkie but don't say anything since he'll be able to hear it from inside."

"You know I have a doctorate, right? I think I can manage the lookout position without blowing your cover," she joked.

Sarah stared ahead at the dashboard for a few moments. "But promise me that you'll be careful."

"I'll be fine. He's asleep anyway. I'm just going in, grabbing the typewriter, and leaving," he said, starting to get out of the car.

"Wait," she said.

Jamie turned toward Sarah, and she leaned over and kissed him. He felt a rush of adrenaline and lingered in the moment.

"If anything goes wrong, get out of there," she said. "It's not worth dying or going to jail for."

He grabbed the small crowbar and climbed out of the car, locking the door behind him. Jamie casually walked down the street toward the World of Intrigue. As soon as the coast was clear, he slipped down the small alleyway between Sebastian's place and the business next door. He hugged the side of the building tightly to stay out of view of the second-floor windows.

A floodlight lit the back of Sebastian's place. Jamie could still see the receipt sticking out between the latch and the doorframe. His plan had worked, and the only remaining obstacle was the door to the hidden office. As Jamie reached to pull on the handle of the back door, he stopped and thought of Sarah, sitting in the car across the street. She was more important than all this, and he contemplated turning around, going back to the car, and leaving this place. Sebastian could have the typewriter and all the power that came with it.

But I'm so close.

He twisted the doorknob and pushed it open.

Jamie wedged the back door open with a piece of scrap metal he found outside and headed into the exhibit room. The smell from the stink bombs was gone now, but the musk of the decaying exhibit remained. The place was eerie at night, and the figures that were so harmless and comical during the day had become ominous shadows reminding Jamie of the shapes that had towered over him during one of his nightmares. He approached the olive-green bookshelves and carefully slid the first one out of the way, attempting to minimize the sound of the squeaky casters. He moved the second, revealing the wooden door behind it. In a futile gesture, Jamie reached out and tried the doorknob. It was locked. *Of course it's still locked.*

He slid the old credit card out of his pocket and wedged it between the doorframe and the door. When it bumped up against the metal latch, Jamie scraped the card against it, trying to slide the lock back into the door. After several minutes, he accidentally broke the card in half. The mechanism on the old door was simply too strong for a flimsy credit card.

It was impossible to do anything with the crowbar without making noise, but Jamie had no choice. He wedged the bar between the door and the frame, next to the handle, and tried to pry it open. The wood made a splintering sound, but the door was thick and heavy, and it wouldn't budge. The harder he pried, the more the wood split and cracked, but the door just wouldn't open.

"This might help," someone said from the darkness.

Jamie spun around, feeling bile rush up his esophagus. He could see the silhouette of a short, round figure, barely lit by the floodlight outside. Sebastian flipped on the light switch so that he could face Jamie. He held a skeleton key in one hand and a revolver in the other. Jamie held a hand out as if to tell Sebastian to wait. Up until that point, his biggest concern was arrest, but he hadn't anticipated a gun.

"Don't worry. I'm not going to shoot you. What I'm going to do, I'm not sure yet. I honestly thought I had a bit more time before you'd come after me. Even thought I might have gotten away with it," Sebastian said.

"Didn't notice any of the cameras then, did you?" Jamie asked. "We sent the footage to the police, and they'll be here any minute."

"I doubt that. You wouldn't be breaking in if you had called the police. We both know that. You're here all by yourself, and nobody knows it," he said.

Sebastian had no idea that Sarah was sitting outside. Surely, she'd see the light from the street. The walkie was tucked in Jamie's back pocket. If only he could reach the button and hint at Sarah to call the police... He heard a frantic pulse of the call button from the other end of the walkie, but Sebastian didn't seem to hear it.

"I see that you've been putting the typewriter to use, with the line around the block today," Jamie said.

"You noticed my boom in business? I simply typed it up, and it came true, just like the rain the other day. That's nothing, though, just the first step in a much larger plan. Surely you—"

The back door swung open with a loud creak. This startled Sebastian, who turned and fired. Jamie saw his only opportunity and threw the crowbar at him, which cracked Sebastian on the back of the head. He stumbled forward and fell flat on his face.

Jamie turned toward the doorway and saw Sarah standing there, holding a hand to her lower stomach. She slid against the doorframe and slumped over on the floor like a rag doll.

"Sarah!" he yelled as he ran toward her.

She gave a soft groan as if she was having a bad dream.

Jamie pulled her head back to see if she was conscious and noticed a large wet patch on her abdomen. "Oh God. Sarah."

She stared at the ceiling with wide eyes, seemingly trying to keep herself awake. Her gaze switched to Jamie, and a look of panic washed over her. "I'm sorry. I saw the light from the street. Thought I could..." she said softly. She closed her eyes, and he could feel hot tears streaming down his face.

As he tried to revive her, Sebastian shuffled on the floor behind him. He coughed, giving Jamie just enough warning to turn and see his eyes opening. The skeleton key had fallen near Jamie's foot, and he twisted to grab it then bolted for the locked door behind the bookshelf. In that instant, he knew what he had to do. He wasn't sure if it would work, but he had to get to the typewriter. Both he and Sarah were screwed if it wasn't locked behind the door to Sebastian's office. As he made it to the door and slid the key into the latch, he heard Sebastian from behind.

"No, no, no!" Sebastian screamed. "Look what you made me do! I di-di-didn't mean to."

Jamie twisted the knob and opened the wooden door just as Sebastian fired a shot into the wooden frame. This caused an explosion of splinters around his head. He managed to make it inside before the next shot and latched the door behind him. The room was dark, and he frantically felt around for the dangling light cord. It brushed the side of his face, and he reached to pull it. The burst of light was blinding at first, but the typewriter quickly came into view, sitting at the center of the makeshift desk. A piece of paper was sitting in the paper feed.

```
People came from all around to see
Sebastian's World of Intrigue.
```

Jamie pulled the carriage return as tears dripped onto the page. He had to think of something, something to save Sarah and something to get them out of there, but she was likely already dead, and the typewriter couldn't just rewrite events from the past. If she was gone, that was all his fault. He should have run from this place back to Sarah and the promise of a fresh start. She had been right when she said that this mystery wasn't his burden. It was T.J.'s burden, and Jamie had willingly put someone he cared about in harm's way to rectify it, just as his uncle had done with him. He'd had a chance to start over, but instead he'd chosen to fall right into his selfish uncle's life, living in his house, surrounded by all the things that he cherished over his family and friends.

But the selfishness stopped now, and Jamie didn't care whether or not he made it out alive. He typed frantically.

```
Jamie  had  another  chance  to  save
her.
```

The first stroke of the axe barely made a dent in the door. The dense wood had been in place for a hundred years at this point, so it wasn't eager to move. As Sebastian struck the door again and again, it started to give way. Jamie stood terrified on the other side. No way would Sebastian allow him to leave, and his only hope was that the typewriter would be able to save Sarah, but it did nothing. She was dead, he feared, and he was doomed to a similar fate. The typewriter sat there.

"You could have just let me have it, like I asked. This is your fault!" Sebastian yelled through the door.

Jamie looked for something to fight with. The metal desk lamp was the best thing he could find. He pulled the lamp cord from the wall and prepared for the door to give way. The room was small, so he had no place to hide. He would have to confront Sebastian head on. He raised the lamp over his head and waited for the stout man to come barreling through the door. The axe pounded against it once more, and Jamie heard something heavy fall to the floor. The door swung open slowly. Sebastian must have hacked away at the latch until there was nothing left to secure the lock to the frame. He stood in the doorway, with the axe lying on the floor next to him and his revolver raised and pointed directly at Jamie.

"I'll be damned if I let you take away my only opportunity to escape from this hellhole," Sebastian said, panting and grunting from overexertion. "I gave my life away to this crap. I'm the one who figured everything out! And what's my reward? Nothing. Well, that ends today."

"All right," Jamie said between sobs. "You can have it. Just let me take her and leave. It's yours. We won't bother you again."

"You and I both know that I can't do that. It's too late now."

Jamie gripped the lamp tightly. He knew he would have only one chance to strike.

"Give me the key," Sebastian said. "I'm going to take you on a tour of the basement."

Jamie picked up the key, sitting next to him on the desk. As Sebastian reached for it, Jamie zipped it toward his face. The key hit Sebastian squarely on the forehead, and Jamie took advantage of the moment. He charged, lamp raised, and swung down on the man, but not before Sebastian squeezed the trigger of the revolver. A blinding flash filled the room, followed by sudden darkness.

CHAPTER TWENTY-EIGHT

J AMIE AWOKE IN A COLD sweat. He fumbled for his phone in the pitch-black room but came up empty-handed. It must have fallen off the nightstand and onto the floor. Jamie lay his head down on the pillow and took a few deep breaths. He turned onto his side and rested his hand on the slumbering form next to him. Her shape slowly expanded and contracted with each breath. He wasn't sure what had just happened nor where reality started and ended, but he was just happy Sarah was alive and sleeping next to him. The late-night raid of Sebastian's shop must have been a paranoid dream.

This whole plan is crazy.

As he calmed down, Jamie resolved to abandon the plan to break into Sebastian's and instead to return to Cincinnati in the morning. Putting Sarah in harm's way wasn't worth it. Losing her wasn't worth it. His heart slowed, and he grew closer and closer to sleep, lulled by the familiar scent of lavender.

The alarm blared, and he clung to the last few moments of sleep. As he rolled over, he was met by a cold and empty bed. *Sarah must have gotten up already.*

Jamie slowly opened his eyes. The room was small, with off-white walls and a nondescript wooden dresser in one corner. He sat up and looked around. He was in the bedroom of his old apartment, the apartment he'd shared with Lilly, the one that was full of memories of dread and loss. He rubbed his eyes with such force that it made his vision blur. This couldn't be real. *Why am I here?*

Jamie walked down the carpeted hallway to the living room, with Buttons following closely behind him. His senses were flooded with sights and smells of old familiar things, things from a previous life that had ended in tragedy. When he saw Lilly's purse on the kitchen table, he felt as if he had been punched in the stomach. As the realization washed over him, he turned back toward the bedroom and ran down the hallway. He searched the bedside table once more for his phone and scooted the table out of the way when he couldn't find it. His cell phone lay between the table and the wall, and he picked it up and unlocked it. Jamie opened the address book on his phone and tapped on one of the names.

A few years had passed, but he could remember the nights that he would call Lilly's voice mail over and over just to hear the sound of her voice. He continued to pay her phone bill just so he could hear it whenever he wanted. In his mind, a chance that she would answer still existed. Although the grieving would never completely go away, he finally cut the service off a year after her death. His fear of forgetting her voice was ill-founded. He would never forget that voice.

"You've reached Lilly. I'm not available right now, but if you leave your name and number, I'll call you back as soon as possible."

Her voice was as sweet and cheerful as it had ever been. Tears came to his eyes. *This is crazy. Lilly is dead!* Jamie checked the date on his phone. *2016. This doesn't make any sense.* The date of Lilly's death was cemented in his brain, but that date hadn't occurred yet, according to his phone.

The day was Tuesday, and Lilly always worked a twelve-hour shift on Tuesdays, usually leaving her phone turned off in her locker. Jamie pulled a set of clothes out of the dresser and threw them on. *But where are my keys?* He stumbled around the apartment for several minutes until he found them under a stack of mail on the counter.

He nearly fell down the steps to the first floor of the complex as he sprinted to the car. The Subaru slid around the corner of the parking lot, and he floored it out onto the street. He'd never driven so fast in his life, and he could feel his head pounding as if his heart was between his eyes. The hospital was only a few miles away, meaning the truth was only a few miles away. Jamie pulled up to the front doors of the hospital, bypassing the parking lot altogether, and jumped out of the car. Lilly would be on the cardiac floor, and he punched the elevator floor button with such force that it stuck for a moment. The doors seemed to take forever to open after the elevator reached the third floor, and Jamie bolted as soon as he had enough room to squeeze his body through. He recognized Bernice, the desk nurse, from the few times he'd had to drop things off for Lilly. She was a sweet older woman, but he had seen her put family members in their places if they stepped out of line.

"Jamie. It's good to see—"

"I have to talk to Lilly," he cut her off before she could finish. He'd lost his breath, but his words came out like bullets.

"Is everything okay?" she asked, picking up the phone and punching in Lilly's pager number.

"I don't know," he replied. He didn't know anything at the moment.

The next few minutes seemed like an eternity, then he saw her appear from around the corner of the hallway. Lilly walked toward Jamie, who was red-faced and visibly emotional.

"What's wrong?" she asked.

Jamie's dead partner was standing in front of him as if nothing had happened. He didn't reply. He couldn't reply. He simply fell to his knees and wept.

CHAPTER TWENTY-NINE

T HE DETAILS OF THE EVENTS leading up to the wreck were fuzzy. Lilly had left her mom's birthday party in the afternoon and began the journey home to Pittsburgh, driving her sporty little red car, which was her first adult purchase after landing a nursing job. Lilly had driven the route home several hundred times before and always got caught at the red light that put her onto the town's main drag. She used the time to call Jamie, to let him know she was on her way, and he knew she'd be home in exactly two hours and fifteen minutes from the call if there wasn't any traffic.

Jamie always thought Lilly was extremely out of place in the little town and had long outgrown it. Still, he noticed she would tear up every time they left.

As Lilly pulled onto the bridge that day, a driver approached in the other direction. Police weren't sure why the other driver swerved into Lilly's lane, but that caused her to slam into the car next to her in an attempt to avoid the oncoming driver. The driver swerved back into their lane and missed her vehicle, but Lilly overcorrected and fishtailed into oncoming traffic.

The wreck went down as one of the worst in the town's history. The local newspaper ran pictures of the twisted metal and debris, and it had been hard to tell that all the scraps had once been cars. Lilly died on impact, but the driver that caused the whole thing fled the scene. He or she either sped off to avoid the trouble or legitimately didn't notice the wreck behind them, which seemed unlikely to Jamie.

Caring for others had been Lilly's life's work, and he found it unfair and sickly ironic that such a lack of care had led to her death. He couldn't bring himself to drive over the bridge to get to her wake and took the long and winding back roads to her parents' house instead. The event was somber with the occasional laugh as family members shared stories of Lilly's childhood. She was mostly a well-behaved kid but had her moments. After tracking mud into the house, she'd decided to use the hose to clean it up, turning the water on and spraying down the floor of the entryway. Her cleaning habits had much improved since then.

Relatives from all over the country filled their plates with ham, deviled eggs, and various forms of potatoes, but Jamie was completely numb to the events around him and isolated himself in a corner armchair. Occasionally, Lilly's father would come over to check on him or a distant relative would offer a few words of sympathy, but he spent most of the time daydreaming about what had been. Months passed before the numbness even began to subside, but it would never completely go away.

Now Jamie, crumpled on the floor of the hospital, stared directly into Lilly's eyes. They were full of life, and the person for whom he had grieved for several years now wrapped her arms around him.

CHAPTER THIRTY

AMIE TRIED TO GO ABOUT his days as he had before Sarah and Turner House, but his mind couldn't make sense of it. He knew he hadn't dreamt the whole thing. His experience had been too vivid, too real to be a dream. Jamie had moved through all the stages of grief and created a new life for himself. His world, which had turned to gray after Lilly's death, was filling with color once again. And Sarah... He felt guilty for even thinking of her now. He hoped she was okay and felt awful for caring so deeply about her when Lilly was right in front of him. But he did care. He could have loved her as he had once loved Lilly... as he did love Lilly. As Sebastian's axe fell on the wooden door, so it fell on Jamie's new life, and he felt the pull between two disparate worlds, one that was and one that could have been.

Lilly clearly knew something was wrong. Jamie hadn't been himself since the incident at the hospital. Whenever she entered the room, he would jump, he barely ate, and he always seemed anxious and preoccupied. This was probably because Jamie *was* anxious and preoccupied. He wanted to tell Lilly all that had happened but had no idea where to begin. So he didn't. He stayed in his head and didn't say a word.

"Don't forget, I'm going to go home for mom's birthday tomorrow," Lilly said. "You can't come, right? Don't you have graduation?"

Jamie was nauseated. The weekend of her horrific car accident had arrived. This was the weekend that would change his life forever. It was the weekend he would replay over and over in his mind, wishing he could have done something to stop it. It would live in his recurring nightmares. In all the shock from recent events, Jamie had forgotten all about the impending crash. He had already lived through losing Lilly, but now he faced her demise once again. The realization hit him like the two-ton car that had crashed into her.

"I don't think you should go," he snapped, causing her to pull back in the chair. He reached for an excuse. "The weather's going to be terrible."

"I have to. I couldn't miss her birthday," she replied. "I know that you have commencement, so I'm okay to go by myself."

He didn't respond. She was strong-willed, and he knew he'd have to plead with her not to go. Part of him had always loved her determination, but now he needed her cooperation.

What about T.J.? The thought came to him out of nowhere. If this was indeed the past, then T.J. was alive and well, probably sitting in his office and scribbling his first draft of Jamie's descent into madness. T.J. had a house phone. Jamie hadn't used it often but did use it enough to remember the number. He was a simple phone call away from the man who could confirm that he wasn't crazy.

He took his phone out of his pocket and stepped outside onto the deck.

"Where are you going?" Lilly asked.

"I have to make a quick call. I'll be right back." He slid the glass door closed and tapped his uncle's number into the dial pad of his phone.

It rang. *At least the number is real.*

It rang again. *Will he even pick up the phone? He isn't exactly sociable.*

"Hello."

Jamie felt a lump in his throat. "Um, yes, T.J.?"

"Can I help you?" the man replied.

"This is Jamie."

There was a pause on the other end.

"It's good to hear from you. What made you decide to call?"

"I think we need to talk about your books, about the typewriter," he replied, his heart racing.

Few additional words were exchanged, but Jamie agreed to come to Turner House tomorrow morning before ending the call.

He came back through the sliding door, and his face was white.

"Are you okay? What's going on?" Lilly asked.

He took a deep breath, sat down at the table across from her, and met her gaze with unblinking focus. She could sense he had been pulled out of his haze, and he was truly with her. He was awake, and she had his full attention.

"I'm sorry. I haven't been myself. I can't explain it now, and there's nothing wrong, but I have to go meet someone tomorrow. I know that you want to go to the party, but you have to make up an excuse. I know that it isn't reasonable to even ask, but you have to trust me. Please, promise me that you won't go. I promise that it will all make sense, and I'll explain everything when I get back."

Lilly wasn't sure what to think, but she nodded her head.

"Promise me. You have to say it."

"I promise," she replied.

His nights had been sleepless, and this one was no different. On the eve of his journey back to Turner House, Jamie lay awake, unable to clear his head. Finally, he abandoned his attempt at sleep altogether and climbed out of bed, the sun still far from peering over the horizon. He walked over to Lilly's side of the bed, leaned over, and kissed her. He still loved her, that much he knew. After one final trip to Turner House, he would put all this to rest. Maybe he could help T.J., but if not, he had to move on, to live in the life he had. He was lucky to be here, to have another chance with her.

Jamie had made the trip to Turner House several times before, but this time was different. The weather was awful. Rain beat down on the Subaru for the entire journey, but something in the white noise was soothing. He was emotionally exhausted, but his thoughts still raced, and the drive felt like an eternity. He had only known T.J. through the artifacts of his life and hadn't talked to the man for many years, but now he would meet him face to face. He passed the truck stop where he'd picked up *Satan's Song*, a moment that felt so far away now.

The gate to the house was open, and the child devil smiled upon the car as he drove through and up the front driveway. Jamie sat and stared for a minute. The place was just as he had remembered it although he'd never actually been there. The memories of his nights in that house, memories of his time with Sarah, all seemed so distant now. He felt guilty for missing her. He cared for her so much and hoped she was okay. However, his time with her was over now. Jamie was straddling two lives, one that lay ahead of him, and one that had ended years ago. He hoped Sarah wouldn't remember any of this so that she didn't have to deal with the pain and confusion he was feeling, at least.

The wooden door of the house creaked open in his periphery. He must have been out of it for a few minutes. A tall well-dressed man stood in the doorway. Jamie felt as if he was seeing a ghost, and based on the look on T.J. Lawson's face, he felt the same way.

CHAPTER THIRTY-ONE

THE WOOD CRACKLED AND HISSED as Jamie stared into the flames. He didn't know where to begin. T.J.'s house was proof that he hadn't dreamt it all. It was just as he remembered, with every knickknack and detail in place. To T.J., Jamie might as well have been a character from one of his books. He'd only known him from a distance and filled in the rest of the details with his imagination.

Jamie had so many questions that he found it difficult to choose one. He and Sarah had worked so hard to figure out the truth behind everything that had happened, and suddenly the source of all the answers was sitting right in front of him.

T.J. broke the silence. "You look just like your dad. I could tell in the pictures, but now that you're in front of me, the resemblance is uncanny."

"Why did you do this to me?" That was the question that bubbled to the surface. "I came here after your death. A friend and I figured out the connection between your books and the real deaths. But Sebastian was insane. We asked him to help us, but he stole the typewriter and shot Sarah.

He killed my friend. He was going to kill me too, but somehow it sent me back here, before any of it happened." Jamie looked T.J. in the eyes. "Why did you do this to me?"

T.J. sat back in his chair for a moment. He rubbed his stubbly chin and seemed to be debating where to begin.

"I'd originally planned to write my third book about this house. There's a fascinating history behind these walls, and I was eager to make something of it... until the letter from Sebastian and the fire that killed Louise. I realized that I was responsible for the deaths of innocent human beings. I was a murderer."

He cupped his hand over his mouth and stared into the fire. "After the tragedies, I lost several years to grief and the paralysis that came with it. I couldn't leave the house or even look in the mirror. Finally, I came to the conclusion, a few weeks ago actually, that I'd end it all. I want to die, to be free of this anguish, but it's my duty to try to fix what I've done first. If I somehow caused these events with the typewriter, then there has to be a way to fix them. I planned... plan to try to rewrite my stories, and if it fails, I'll allow myself to end the suffering. I can't stop the memories from replaying over and over in my head, but the promise of eventual reprieve has made them more bearable."

Jamie knew T.J. had shut himself off from the outside world, but he had even seemed to lock parts of his mind away from himself.

"But why would you bring me into all of this?" Jamie asked.

"You are my backup plan. If my plans fail, I'd hoped that you might be able to figure things out," T.J. replied.

"So you forced my hand? You made me come here to fix something that was your fault to begin with because you were too big of a coward to live with what you'd done?" Jamie was clenching the edges of the chair.

"You should have heard your dad talk about you. He was so proud. I talked to him every week or so, and we'd mostly talk about you. Although we'd only met when you were little, it felt like I watched you grow up. If my plan to rewrite my stories fails, I want to ensure that I leave all of this in the hands of someone who just might figure out how to make things better. If you're anything like your father, I know that you won't quit until you figure it out. And the fact that you're here says that you've done a damn fine job."

"Like my dad? My dad wouldn't endanger people that he loved in order to fix his stupid mistakes. My friend died because of you, because we were chasing after that stupid typewriter," Jamie said.

"You're only partially correct," T.J. replied. "I just brought you here. Haven't you seen what happens when I write other people's stories for them? I think I've caused enough suffering in my lifetime. I just wanted to get you here. From there, it would be up to you. I hoped that I could count on you, and I had to trust that you'd figure the rest out. I didn't want to write you into something that you had no control over. I couldn't be responsible for another death. I was planning to leave my journal to lead you in the right direction, but you chose to go chasing after the typewriter. I didn't write that. You could have simply turned around and gone back home, so anything that came as a result of your actions is your doing."

The last sentence hit Jamie in the gut. He thought back to the World of Intrigue. He had chosen to sneak in even though he wanted to run back to Sarah and leave the mystery behind. But he didn't. He chose the mystery over someone for whom he cared deeply. Maybe he wasn't like his dad at all. T.J. had been wrong about that. His dad wouldn't have done this. Jamie realized that his anger towards T.J. was actually self-loathing for the decisions he had made.

"What about the manuscript then? Why burn it if you planned this all along? We found pieces of it in the fireplace," Jamie asked.

"I hadn't planned on burning it. My only guess is that I didn't want to risk someone else finding it and trying to publish it," he replied.

Jamie was able to fill in a lot of the gaps in the story by piecing together the bits and bobs of his experiences, but he had one big question he was still unable to answer.

"Where did the typewriter come from?"

CHAPTER THIRTY-TWO

T.J. DIDN'T NOTICE THE HUM of the conveyer belts anymore. The sound had become a part of him, just like his beating heart. The year was 1977, and he sat on a manufacturing line, building circuit boards for television sets. Although he had managed to finish high school, he had no aspirations of going to college. *What for?*

At twenty years old, he'd reached the peak of his manufacturing career. Every day was the same, filled with endless wiring and soldering. Relief finally came in the form of the Japanese electronics industry, which poured well-made and inexpensive televisions into the US market and put his company out of business. He watched as the lines closed down and the less effective employees slowly disappeared from the plant floor. Finally, nothing was left to consolidate, and the company folded. That left him without a job in a sea of unemployed line workers, but no companies were left to turn to, and he had little motivation to continue doing something he hated.

The days blended together and passed with little forward motion. T.J. lived in an apartment with one of his high-school buddies, Ronan, and they picked up odd jobs around the neighborhood mowing lawns, painting houses, and fixing broken appliances. While T.J. spent his days in a state of consistent intellectual boredom, he spent his evenings in the midst of ghosts, demons, and murderers. Something about the thrill of the unknown and supernatural made him feel alive. He first discovered the works of Stephen King through his book *Carrie*, but T.J. had little in common with a pubescent high schooler with a crazy mother and supernatural abilities. Still, something about the storytelling pulled him in, making him relate to the main character.

The bookstore was his salvation from the life he had created, and he spent hours scouring the shelves for anything that could deliver another hit of adrenaline. On one particular day, he noticed a new book from King, front and center on one of the shelves. Two things about the cover drew him in. The first was that he himself looked surprisingly like the character on the dust jacket, with dark-brown hair, an elongated nose, and a distinct jaw. The second was the menacing hotel that sat in the background. Son, husband, and wife were superimposed over the white building, which was framed as if it were another character in the story. He had to have it.

The landlord kept the apartment complex a few degrees above freezing, and T.J. kept his blood flowing with the help of his grandma's hand-sewn quilt and the occasional nip from a bottle of Jim Beam. He found respite from the cold behind the doors of the massive hotel in the book, along with the characters who had settled in for a long winter. He had a fascination with the intricacies of a story's setting and set pieces, and the author painstakingly explored every nook and cranny of the hotel. T.J. read the entire book in three days and immediately reread it a second time. He had completely forgotten about his aimless life and his empty stomach and did everything he could to inhabit this new world for as long as possible. The terror kept him in the present moment, and all his other worries seemed to fade away. Eventually, he added the book to his shelf of well-worn adventures, but it left an itch behind, an itch he couldn't scratch with the trashy old trade paperbacks he was accustomed to or with the booze that warmed his blood.

T.J. spent the day with Ronan, painting the house of one of Ronan's aunts. Bridget owned a brick shotgun home in desperate need of a fresh coat of paint. T.J. stood on the scaffolding and marveled at the difference as he rolled over the splotchy white with a coat of deep red. He carefully etched around the window frame, but something caught his eye on the other side of the glass. As Bridget entered the bedroom, she tripped over the rug and fell into the dresser, hitting her head.

"Ronan!" he yelled as he pushed open the window from the outside, knocking over the paint tray in the process. The sill was just high enough to make the climb a challenge, but he managed to pull himself up and tumble through the window and into the house. Ronan, who heard the commotion from the front porch, threw open the front door. His aunt lay motionless on the floor of the bedroom but came to after a few moments of terror. They spent the afternoon at the hospital, but fortunately Bridget escaped with only a mild concussion and was permitted to go home.

Ronan decided to stay the night after tucking his aunt into bed, and T.J. offered to keep him company. Bridget told the boys to take a few dollar bills from the teapot above the sink and treat themselves to dinner. They picked up a large pizza and still had enough left over for a six pack of beer. They brought their feast back to the house and sat out on the front porch, telling stories and shooting the breeze. Once the sun went down, they went inside, where Ronan swiftly passed out on the couch.

T.J. was too wired from the day's events to sleep. He had just enough of a buzz to quiet his discontent, and he looked around the living room for a source of entertainment. Bridget's bookshelf consisted of a few versions of the Bible and an encyclopedia. He snooped around the bottom floor and sat at her desk, on which sat an old adding machine, a legal pad, and a dull pencil. He flipped the yellow pad over to a fresh page and picked up the pencil. He sharpened its dull point with his pocket knife and put it to paper.

> Jim looked out of the window and into the apartment across the alleyway. The woman sat at the vanity and applied a thick dusting of white powder to her face. She turned her head toward the doorway and stood as the door opened slowly to reveal a figure whose face was covered with some kind of black bag. Startled, she took a step backward and tripped over her chair, hitting her head on the edge of the vanity. The figure's head shot upward, and Jim could feel the glare of its eyes through the slipshod mask. He immediately dropped to the floor and hid below the window frame.

T.J. scribbled out an entire short story onto the legal pad. It exploded from his fingertips as if it had been building up pressure in the back of his brain, waiting for the opportunity to escape. It happened in a flash, and he pushed back the chair to admire his work. Some of the sentences were awkward, and the entire thing was rough around the edges, but the feeling of creation was invigorating. Up until that point, T.J. had relied on other people to create the worlds to which he escaped, but this time, he had created his own. The time was three in the morning when he finished, and he laid his head down at the desk and slept until sunshine crept through the window and onto his face.

His mind had twisted the events of the day into what would become one of his only published works outside of the *Dreadful Objects* books. He submitted it to several pulp magazines under Ronan's encouragement. The rejection letters came pouring in until one magazine made an offer to buy the story for two hundred dollars, which was a significant amount in 1977.

"What are you going to do with the money?" Ronan asked as they sat around the kitchen table, staring at the check.

T.J. had never had that much money before. His poverty kept him trapped in the city, so he was determined to use part of the proceeds to escape for a while.

"I was thinking we could take a road trip up to Colorado," he replied.

"What the hell's in Colorado?" Ronan asked.

"There are mountains, first of all," he said.

"Never seen mountains," Ronan said. "At least, never seen 'em in person."

"There's also the hotel from that book that I've been talking about. I read this interview with the author, and he mentions that the inspiration for the book came while he stayed at this place in Colorado. I was thinking that we could go there and check it out—make a trip of it, you know?"

T.J. didn't have a car at the time, but they borrowed Bridget's '64 Oldsmobile Deluxe. She was virtually blind and wouldn't be needing it anytime soon. They loaded up a cooler with some sandwiches and a few beers and hit the road. As they left Cincinnati, "Hotel California" blared on the radio. Ronan was just happy to escape the city for a while, but he still felt bad about letting T.J. foot the bill for the excursion.

Although T.J. was poor, Ronan was destitute. Several times, T.J. had had to float him rent money, but Ronan didn't blow his paycheck on cigarettes or anything like that. Every two weeks, he brought a legal envelope full of cash to his mom. His father had died when he was a little boy, and his stepfather was an alcoholic who'd passed away and left his mother with little more than her name. He remembered one Christmas when his stepdad had brought home a can of spray snow. Instead of spraying it on the Christmas tree, he ended up spraying it all over the walls of the house. Ronan thought that was funny at the time, and he didn't realize until his teens why his mom never laughed at the drunken behavior.

Getting to Colorado took a few days, but the time passed quickly. They drove in shifts, stopping every once in a while to take in a roadside attraction. They came up through the Town of Estes Park via US Route 36, and the hotel sat right outside of

Rocky Mountain National Park. Ronan pulled into the parking lot of the hotel, and they walked to the front to take it all in. It was an imposing white building with a brownish-red roof. The hotel stay would wipe out most of T.J.'s remaining cash from the magazine, but it was worth it.

He could almost see the author walking the halls and standing in the lobby. The dimly lit hotel seemed like a place stuck in time, with historic wallpaper and furniture. A placard sat at the bottom of the grand staircase and read Hotel Guests Only Please. Apparently, they weren't the first tourists looking for a glimpse of the author's inspiration. Several other people were scattered throughout the lobby, admiring the pictures on the walls and taking in the decor.

T.J. noticed Ronan eyeing the impressive bar. "Buy you a drink?" T.J. asked Ronan, who moved toward an empty set of bar stools.

All that was missing was a spectral bartender.

After exploring the hotel, they stopped at a small diner outside town. The laminated menus were humongous and filled with various greasy dishes. The day's drive had been exhausting, and they sat and ate in relative silence. T.J. looked out the window and across the street. Not much was around, but he noticed a small antiques shop across the way.

"Lola's Odds and Ends. What a weird name for a store," he said. "We should check it out after we eat."

Lola's Odds and Ends was a small one-floor building in the middle of a vacant asphalt parking lot. It was comically tiny, compared to the huge lot that surrounded it. A neon Open sign hung in the window.

Lola stood at the counter, reading a cheap paperback romance. She must have been about sixty years old and wore a jet-black wig and horn-rimmed glasses. She had a Bettie Page meets Vampira look about her, and her face was painted pale, with violet shading on her cheekbones and eyelids.

"Help you?" she asked halfheartedly, casually glancing up from her book.

"Just looking around, thanks," T.J. replied.

The tiny shop was packed with old furniture, vintage clothing, and knickknacks.

"This place is great," he said, running his fingers along the wooden etchings of an old grandfather clock.

He and Ronan worked their way to the back of the store, which was reserved for tattered clothes and broken mementos. T.J. passed old watches with cracked glass, faded garments, and broken appliances before noticing an old Royal typewriter sitting behind a set of chipped glasses. It reminded him of his dad's typewriter, which he used to play with as a child, but this one was much older. His dad's had been a common secretarial typewriter from World War II, but this one looked as if it was from the turn of the century.

"See something you like?"

He was so enamored with the object that he hadn't noticed Lola standing behind him. "Jesus!" he replied as he twisted around with a startled jump.

"Can't help you with that unless you're into velvet paintings. We have a few of those," she said, pointing toward the other corner of the store.

He couldn't tell if she was joking. "Sorry, just caught me off guard. What can you tell me about this typewriter?" He asked.

"Not much, unfortunately. I picked it up at an estate sale a few months ago. The owner was a businessman of some sort. You should have seen the house, though. It was gorgeous! I bought this thinking that I could fix it, but I haven't had the time to look at it." Clearly, Lola had been very busy tending to her invisible customers. She walked over and pressed one of the keys. It made it halfway to the carriage and jammed.

"The mechanisms are all out of whack, but it probably won't be too hard to fix if you're mechanically inclined."

"How much do you want for it?" He asked.

"Five dollars for you, honey," she replied. "But only because I like you."

Ever since he'd sold his original story, T.J. had to rely on cheap notepads and pencils or to go to the library anytime he wanted to type. He had grand visions of himself clacking away at his own typewriter, perched upon the kitchen card table in his apartment.

He slid the old leather wallet from his back pocket, unfolded it, and pulled out a crisp five-dollar bill. Maybe he wouldn't be able to fix it, but the gamble was worth five bucks.

T.J. and Ronan stayed the night in the hotel and soaked in the mountains for another afternoon before heading back to Cincinnati. Getting the typewriter working again took T.J. several days of tinkering. He thought that decades of grit and grime might have mucked up the inner workings, but it was pristine inside. He applied a liberal amount of grease, but the keys still refused to make contact with the carriage. Then he noticed several small metal pins laced in between the key mechanisms as if they had been put there on purpose. He pulled them out with a set of needle-nose pliers.

He fed a piece of paper through the carriage and pulled the carriage return, which made a satisfying *thwack*. The ribbon must have been old because it left nothing more than a faint outline of the letter. He would have to pick up a new ribbon.

T.J. would need several years to publish his first novel, *Satan's Song*. Ronan had gotten himself a job as a press operator at a local printer, and he managed to get T.J. a gig as a maintenance man. T.J. would come home from work and type away, sitting at the folding table in his apartment, just as he had imagined.

CHAPTER
THIRTY-THREE

J AMIE'S EYES WERE WIDE. "So that's it? Did you ever find out more about it?"

"By the time I figured out what was going on, the antique shop was closed, and Lola was dead," T.J. said. "I didn't have enough information to track down the original owner. The trail was cold, and all I could do was try to correct my mistakes. I obtained the film reel from Louise's son and locked the objects away. I thought that maybe they'd cause more damage, but they're harmless," T.J. said.

"All of the power comes from the typewriter, from the stories that it infuses into the objects, not the objects themselves," Jamie added. "There's nothing special about them, now that their stories are over."

"Precisely," T.J. said.

Jamie had wondered why the objects never gave him any trouble. They were useless hunks of junk because their power came from elsewhere.

"I think that I may have figured out why your plan isn't going to work," he said.

"How?" T.J. asked.

"'Jamie had another chance to save her.' It was the last thing that I typed before Sebastian pulled the trigger. Somehow, that was enough to dump me back here. I woke up in the bed in my old apartment, right next to Lilly, before her car crash."

"I've wracked my brain over what to do, and you're telling me that I just have to type, 'It was all a dream,' and it'll fix everything?" T.J. asked.

"It wasn't a dream, and it isn't that simple. Do you have a piece of paper and something to write with? Wait, I can just get it myself." Jamie walked over to the table by the door and pulled the notepad and pencil out of the drawer.

He'd spent the drive to Turner House building a theory in his head about how the typewriter worked. It might have been crazy, but it was at least a starting point. T.J. watched intently as Jamie drew an arrow across the page.

"This is our timeline," he said. "If you try to rewrite the ending to *Satan's Song*, you're asking the typewriter to change the past." He drew another arrow under the first, parallel but with the tip going in the opposite direction.

"And it won't work?" T.J. asked.

"Right, it can't change the past. But, somehow, it took me back here, took me into the past and left me with all the memories from my time in Turner House. I didn't ask it to change anything—I asked it to take me back here so that I could change it myself. I didn't know that this is what I was asking for, but somehow it's how the thing interpreted my request." He drew a semicircle from the head of the arrow back to the base. "And I guess from here, it's up to us." He drew another arrow from the base of the first, but in a slightly different direction. "It's like we have the opportunity to create a new path, or at least I think we do."

"But why did it bring you back here? If you were trying to save your friend, why would it take you this far back?"

Jamie thought back to the moment.

"Because I wasn't just thinking about her," he replied. "I read the line, and I wrote it for Sarah, but it reminded me of Lilly too. It's like it knew what I was thinking."

"Just like I was thinking about Louise McAulle when I wrote *Cellulose*," T.J. replied. "But what about *Satan's Song*? I made the whole thing up."

Jamie remembered the day when he, Sarah, and Sebastian tested the typewriter. "Sarah said something about the stories sticking to those who were similar. If you weren't thinking of anyone in particular, maybe it just found the closest match to the characters in your story. Emily had enough in common with Annabelle, and the typewriter must have simply made the connection. I don't completely understand it, but maybe the fit was just close enough to work."

CHAPTER THIRTY-FOUR

THE TYPEWRITER SAT ON THE writing desk, just as Jamie remembered it. T.J. poured two glasses of bourbon at the bar and set one next to him. T.J.'s fingers ran along the back edge of the leather wingback chair. He had spent many hours in it, causing immeasurable amounts of chaos. Now Jamie had taken the reins and would make up for the mess that he had made. If Jamie had somehow managed to erase his own life at Turner House, then he should be able to do the same for T.J.

The trick wasn't trying to rewrite what the typewriter had already cemented into place. No, it was to go back and fix things in person, to create a new path forward without the death and devastation. T.J.'s victims could still be saved, and Jamie knew exactly what he needed to type in order to do it.

Jamie sat in the chair and took a swig of bourbon with T.J. standing behind him. It burned as it went down, but the burn brought him to life. The keys tapped out a rhythm on the page as he typed.

```
T.J.  had  another  chance  to  save
those whose lives he'd affected with
the typewriter.
```

It was a simple sentence to address several decades of misery. Jamie sat back in the chair as T.J. peered over his shoulder.

"When will we know if it worked?" he asked.

"You'll know when you wake up tomorrow morning. I don't know what this means for me. Maybe I won't remember anything. I assume the same thing happened to Sarah," he replied.

As they returned downstairs to the living room, Jamie picked up his phone from the coffee table and noticed the flashing notification light. A message from Lilly greeted him as the screen switched on.

```
I'm  going  to  leave  Mom's  soon.
I  decided  that  I  couldn't  miss
the  party.  I  know  that  you  won't
understand,  but  I  couldn't  just
abandon  my  family  for  no  good
reason.  I'll  be  back  tonight,  and
maybe we can talk then. And I think
that  we  need  to  have  a  serious
conversation.
```

He could feel the hairs on the back of his neck stand on end and looked at the time on his phone, 3:30 p.m. The crash had occurred at 3:13. His efforts to keep Lilly from attending the party had been futile. She'd gone anyway, and if things played out as they had before, she had died exactly seventeen minutes ago. He frantically tapped on her name to call. The phone rang... and rang... and rang... but nobody answered.

"You have to stay where you are. Don't go anywhere!" he shouted into the phone when her voice mail clicked in. He tapped the same message out via text too. Maybe he had time to save her. Maybe things were just different enough to prevent the accident this time.

He searched for her mom's number, hit it, and held the phone to his ear.

"Hello," she answered.

"This is Jamie," he said in barely intelligible words. "Is Lilly still there?"

"She left a few minutes ago. Is everything—"

He hung up before she had a chance to finish her sentence.

"She went to the party and just left," he said, rubbing his forehead in anguish. He thought for a moment then ran toward the stairs.

"Typewriter!" he yelled as T.J. followed.

Jamie frantically pulled the carriage return and typed a new line.

```
Lilly's  car  stalled  before  she
pulled onto the bridge.
```

"Is that enough?" he shouted. As he stepped back from the typewriter, the full realization of what was happening started to sink in. *I missed her. I abandoned her for this stupid story, just like Sarah, and now she's dead.*

"I killed her," he said.

He could feel his pulse pounding between his eyes. Darkness started at the corner of his vision and slowly crept in as if he had gotten up too quickly. Before he knew it, Jamie couldn't see anything. He tried to stabilize himself but fell against the cabinet behind the desk, knocking a ceramic figure to the floor, which shattered on impact. T.J. rushed to his side and braced him so that he could fall to the floor without injuring himself.

"Breathe! Take deep breaths," T.J. said, but Jamie had already passed out.

CHAPTER THIRTY-FIVE

J AMIE LAY IN SOMETHING COLD but needed a moment to realize the liquid creeping down his arm was his own blood. He lifted his head to see a hooded figure standing over him. As he tried to scream, it lurched forward and pulled him up by his collar, lifting him from the floor until his feet no longer touched the ground. The being's face was obscured by the shadow from its hood, and in a moment of bravery, Jamie gripped the fabric and pulled it away from the figure's head. Its face had no semblance of humanity, aside from a set of gnashing teeth, which were chipped and yellowed. Its skin was riddled with deep scars, and dark pockets sat where the eyes should have been. As it brought him closer to its face, Jamie's body relaxed. Now that he could see the true form of the monster that had been chasing him, it wasn't something worthy of his fear. He pitied the creature, deformed by grief and treachery, defined by what once had been.

At this moment of clarity, something wrapped around Jamie's waist, pulling him free from its grip and into a bright sunburst. He felt the warm glow, which started on his face and grew until it overcame his entire body.

The sun danced across the room as the curtains fluttered from a breeze coming through the cracked window. His mind sat once again between sleep and the waking world. The recent events had yet to come flowing back into his consciousness. For a moment, he was free. Jamie opened his eyes, and the twirling ceiling fan came into focus. He rolled over to his left side and saw Lilly lying next to him, body softly rising and falling with every breath. Then his memory came rushing back. He sat upright in the bed and kicked Buttons off his feet. The pup groaned in displeasure and jumped down onto the hardwood floor.

"What's wrong?" Lilly asked, half asleep.

"Nothing. Go back to sleep," he replied.

She rolled onto her stomach and pulled the sheet up over her shoulders.

Jamie checked the date on his phone. It was still the day of the accident. *But how did I get back here? How many times will I have to relive this day? What happened to T.J.?* He walked out to the living room, sat at the kitchen bar, and dialed T.J.'s number.

"The number that you have dialed is no longer in service," a recording said over the line.

Am I losing my mind?

Lilly came down the hallway and into the kitchen, wearing an oversized T-shirt with a Lichtenstein print on it. He loved it when she wore nothing but a T-shirt in the mornings.

"I'm going with you today," he said.

"I thought that you had to go to graduation today," she replied.

"I'll just tell them that I'm sick and can't make it." He wasn't sure exactly what was happening, but he knew the only way to be certain she would return home in one piece would be to go with her. He couldn't chance leaving her behind to venture to T.J.'s, and no way was he going to let her out of his sight again.

Jamie put Buttons on the leash and took him down to the front courtyard. The cool spring air blew through his hair as he walked the dog along the hedgerows. Spring brought a sense of renewal and with it another chance at redemption. After the walk, they went back upstairs, and he grabbed the overnight bag Lilly had packed for them. He loaded the bag and the dog into the car, and Lilly came out of the complex, carrying two travel mugs of coffee.

"Let's hit the road," she said, closing the passenger-side door. "I'm glad that you decided to come."

"Me too," he replied. "I'd much rather be with you than at school. They'll live without me." He couldn't say the same for her. He had no idea what the day had in store, but he knew she stood a much better chance if he was with her.

Jamie was on autopilot, doing barely more than keeping the car on the road. Lilly tried to make small talk, but he wasn't having any of it. He would nod in response, but his mind was elsewhere.

"What's wrong?" she asked, breaking fifteen minutes of solid silence.

"Nothing, babe," he replied. "Everything's fine."

"It's clearly not fine. You've barely said a word this entire trip. I can tell that something's bothering you. Did I do something?"

Jamie broke his gaze with the road, glanced at Lilly, and then brought his eyes back to the road. He struggled to find words that would make sense.

"No, I'm sorry," he said. "It's not you at all."

"Then what is it?"

"I just have a weird feeling. It's just been a stressful week." That wasn't a lie. He did have a feeling in the pit of his stomach, and it had been a stressful week, but he couldn't tell Lilly everything. The truth was too crazy to believe. He put his hand on her leg and squeezed.

"I love you," he said.

"I love you too." She smiled.

They reached the top of the hill looking down on the bridge into the city. So many emotions were tied to this place now. The last time Jamie had been here had been in a previous life, to attend the funeral of someone he loved so deeply that he nearly crawled into the grave with her. He had dreamed of this bridge and lain in the metal wreckage that ripped through his psyche and embedded itself into the back of his brain. And now, he was sitting next to his lost love, but it somehow felt like a dream, temporary and fleeting. He had spoken to T.J. the day before, had just relived this tragedy, but here he sat once again, on the day his life would change forever.

Jamie opened the window for some fresh air, just enough so that the dog could stick his head out into the air stream. He found it difficult not to visualize the images of the wreck in the newspaper. Jamie took a deep breath and exhaled loudly. Relief came when the car crossed over the expansion joint and onto the other side of the bridge.

CHAPTER THIRTY-SIX

ILLY'S CAR SLUMPED SADLY IN her mom's driveway. Someone had slashed the tires on the left side as the family celebrated inside. Clearly, whoever had done it had a vested interest in Lilly staying put for a while.

Her mom called the police, but they couldn't send an officer for a few hours. She watched Buttons pacing on the stone wall in the backyard, sniffing out the chipmunks hidden between the rocks, while Lilly and Jamie sat at the kitchen table with the officer.

"Any idea of who could have done this?" The officer asked. Jamie knew who did it but remained tight-lipped. He had simply planned to take the backroads out of town and avoid the bridge, but T.J. apparently had other ideas in mind. This meant that he must have been in the area or perhaps paid someone to slash Lilly's tires. Jamie's plan to send T.J. back must have worked, but Jamie wondered what happened to the subjects of his first two books. *Was he able to save them?*

"No idea, and no one around here saw anything," Lilly replied. "I just don't get it."

"Probably just kids causing trouble," the officer replied. He finished the report and gave it to Lilly to sign.

She scrawled her name on the signature line.

Then he packed up and headed toward the door. "We'll let you know if we find anything. I wouldn't expect much to come from it, but we'll send you a copy of the report to send to your insurance company."

"I'm so glad that you're here with me," Lilly said, wrapping her arms around Jamie.

"Me too," he said, resting his chin on the top of her head.

"Maybe Mom should get a security system," she said.

"I'm sure it'll be fine. You heard him. It was probably just a few kids. Maybe your mom just pissed off the wrong ones or something," he said.

"Well, she did get her house egged after she refused to give a few trick-or-treaters candy last year. Said they were 'too old,'" she replied.

"See, it's probably the same brats. There's nothing to worry about."

The tow-truck driver loaded the car onto the flatbed, and Lilly spent the afternoon on the phone with the insurance company. The car would be fixed by the end of the day, and they would be able to go home and sleep in their own beds.

Jamie felt a sense of relief wash over him. Lilly was safe, and now he had assurance that she would be nowhere near the bridge during the time of the accident.

Once the car was ready to pick up, Lilly's mom dropped them at the mechanic. Jamie looked at his watch. The repair shop had had a slow day, so they were able to fix the car much more quickly than expected, but the time was already five minutes or so past the accident. It was over, and Lilly was still alive. They would finally be able to put this day behind them once and for all. Jamie was ready to move on.

"Want to drop in and see your uncle on the way back?" she asked.

Jamie thought he'd misheard and gave Lilly a strange look.

"Okay, just a thought," she said defensively.

As he drove away from the city and toward the bridge out of town, a blaring police siren approached from behind. His eyes flashed down to the speedometer. *Thank God.* The speed limit was fifty-five, and he was going fifty-seven. He pulled over to the side of the road to let the vehicle pass. It blew by him and was quickly followed by another cruiser.

"What the hell's going on?" Lilly asked.

A moment later, they noticed a fire truck in the rearview and pulled over again—fire truck, police car, police car, ambulance.

As he reached the edge of town, Jamie saw thick black smoke billowing from the bridge. A line of cars extended up the hill, and some had started to turn around. Police barricades blocked the road completely, about a half mile up the road.

He felt a knot forming in the pit of his stomach and pulled the car over into the emergency lane.

"What are you doing?" she asked.

"Stay here," he replied as he opened the car door and stepped outside to get a better look.

A helicopter circled overhead, and a dozen or so emergency response vehicles were surrounding the area.

It happened without her.

Jamie sprinted down the road toward the bridge.

"Where the hell are you going?" Lilly yelled after him, but he was already long gone.

Jamie could see the cluster of police cars and fire trucks surrounding the scene of the crash. The entrance to the bridge was barricaded, as was the entrance on the other end.

Bright yellow flames shot up from an overturned tanker in the center of the bridge, and an SUV lay on its side, next to the large truck. The car appeared to have been ripped apart, and shredded metal and debris lay scattered across the pavement.

Jamie was going to be ill. He couldn't breathe and fell to his knees. They'd managed to save Lilly once and for all, but someone else paid the price for it. *How could I have been so stupid?*

Lilly witnessed Jamie's breakdown from the car. When he fell to the ground, she turned on the emergency lights and got out to comfort him. The dog barked anxiously as he watched her run toward Jamie.

She bent down to embrace him.

"It's all my fault," he said. "I killed them."

She held Jamie for several minutes but didn't seem to catch what he'd said. Eventually, she led him back to the car. Lilly assumed driving duties and decided to take the back roads out of town.

Jamie was inconsolable.

"Babe, it's okay," she said. "We don't even know what happened. Maybe they were able to get out. Why are you freaking out so much about this?"

"Because it's my fault," he muttered softly under his breath.

"Your fault? What are you talking about?"

"I killed them. They're dead because of me," he said.

"You're not making any sense. You had nothing to do with this. You're freaking me out a little," she replied.

Jamie sat in silence, but his mind was hard at work.

How am I going to fix this? Although he didn't have an answer, he knew the truth sat on a desk in Turner House. It still wasn't over, and he would have to go back one more time. The thought made him want to vomit.

Lilly had driven the back roads several times but never with this level of traffic. Weaving through town and out the other side took her half an hour. Apparently, everyone else had the same plan.

CHAPTER THIRTY-SEVEN

J AMIE SPED TOWARD TURNER HOUSE and his only chance of stopping the crash. His head spun as he tried to reason through what he would need to do. Maybe he could go back one more time although he had no idea how he could prevent the accident, short of shutting down the bridge. He knew some solution existed behind the keys of the typewriter, but he wondered how many more times he could relive the day and what if this time he made the situation even worse.

The Subaru tires slid on the gravel as he pulled into the driveway, but the gate was shut and chained. He contemplated ramming the car through but doubted it could tear open the heavy wrought iron. Jamie hopped out of the car and looked up at the gate. The bars were tall and skinny, with little more to grab onto than the decorative filigree at the top of each spindle. He wasn't in the best shape but managed to step on the lower bar and give himself enough of a boost to make it up and over the top.

He lost his balance and fell over into the bushes on the other side. The bush branches scratched and scraped at his arms, but their cushion prevented more serious injury.

Jamie rolled out of the bush and onto the grass. The blades were long and unkempt. As he stood and looked up at the house, he was surprised by the structure that met his gaze. The garden, once constructed with clean lines and sculpted beds, now sat sloppy and overgrown. The house was in a similar state. The paint was faded and chipping, and several wooden shingles lay scattered on the front lawn.

He walked up the steps, which creaked under his weight. The doorknob hung limp on the door, and he jiggled it, causing it to come loose and fall to the ground. It was merely decoration at this point, but the padlock that had replaced the deadbolt was locked tight. The lights were off inside, and he saw no signs of movement. Jamie stood back and lifted his right leg. He slammed it as hard as he could against the solid wood door, which barely budged.

So much for kicking it in. The TV shows made it seem a lot easier than this, and he thought he might have pulled a muscle in the process.

Jamie walked around the porch to the back of the house and tried the back door, but it was locked tight as well. He looked around the yard for a hard object to break one of the glass door panels and found a loose stone next to the wooden steps. The rock shattered the glass on impact, and he carefully reached through the broken panel to unlatch the door. The house was dark and looked as though it had been empty for years. The moonlight shone through the windows, casting an eerie shadow on the decrepit interior.

Jamie walked along the kitchen cabinets, one hand tracing the marble countertop. He felt for the light switch next to the kitchen door and pressed it, but nothing happened. Fortunately, he had brought a small pocket flashlight, which he twisted on as he walked into the main hallway. The LED light washed over the walls, and Jamie was surprised to see the hallway empty. The shelves and racks of jars and movie memorabilia were all gone, and the walls were bare. Everything that had reminded him of T.J. was missing. The living room was the same, full of old dusty furniture but devoid of the character of its former inhabitant.

The grand staircase was long and ominous, and the light from his small flashlight only made it halfway to the top. He had climbed this set of stairs a hundred times before, but this time, he was afraid of what he might find—or not find—at the other end. He gripped the handrail and started to climb. The doors to T.J.'s office were ajar and off their metal casters, so sliding them out of the way took some effort. The grand desk was still there although it had been covered with a sheet. Jamie expected to see the typewriter sitting in the center of the desk as it always had been. Indeed, he could make out the edges of an object beneath the sheet.

In one sweeping motion, he ripped the sheet off the desk, sending a cloud of dust into the atmosphere. The shape underneath the sheet hadn't been a typewriter at all but rather a stack of old books. This wasn't T.J.'s desk either. He looked around the room, but no typewriter was in sight—no object cases either. *What the hell is going on?*

The sound of a creaking door on the first floor startled him. At first, he thought that might have just been the wind until he heard the distinct sound of floorboards bending under the weight of heavy boots.

"Police. If there's anybody in here, say so now."

"Shit," Jamie said under his breath. He contemplated ways of escape. He could climb out the window, but the drop to the ground below was pretty far, one that even the bulky typewriter had failed to survive. His mind rushed to think of a story, and he looked around for some source of last-minute salvation.

"Come out now!" The command came from the base of the stairs and was more forceful this time.

"I'm up here! I'm coming down the stairs!" Jamie yelled as he walked toward the staircase.

Shuffling was audible below. "Come down slowly, with your hands in front of you," the person responded.

Jamie descended the staircase as two officers watched intently. The difference in stature between the two officers would have been comical if not for the gravity of the situation. One of the men was tall and beefy while the other was short and stout. The tall officer grabbed Jamie's wrist and cuffed his hands behind his back.

They led Jamie outside to the front of the house. Two SUV police cruisers were parked on the other side of the fence, blocking in Jamie's car. He was thankful he hadn't tried to escape, for he would have had nowhere to go. Surrender was the best option. They sat him in the back of the police cruiser.

"I think that there's a misunderstanding. I came here to find my uncle." In a panic to find a lie that would explain his presence, he resolved to tell the truth. He wasn't quite sure what the truth was anymore, but he had no more room left inside himself for lies or deception. "Have someone check the owner of the house. I swear. T.J. Lawson is my uncle."

"Where's your wallet, son?" the officer asked.

"In my back pocket," he replied.

The man reached into the car and pulled Jamie's wallet out of his pocket. He slid the driver's license out of the protective sleeve and took a look.

"Hold on a minute," he said as he shut the door to the cruiser.

Jamie wasn't exactly sure how he could "hold on" since he had nowhere to go, but he was hopeful this little bit of info would make a difference.

The officer walked over to the second cruiser and spoke to the other, who was scribbling something down on a notepad. They had a brief exchange, and Jamie saw the first officer point at his ID and then at the house. He turned around and leaned on the side of the cruiser, grabbed his walkie-talkie, and spoke into it. A few moments passed, then he walked back over to the car.

"When's the last time you spoke with your uncle?" the officer asked.

"Just today," he replied. However, at this point, Jamie had relived the day three times.

"Son, nobody's lived in this house for years, and you certainly aren't the first person we've caught snooping around."

Jamie panicked. "Um, I know." He reached for a response that wasn't absurd. "My uncle's not well. He owns this house. I know he hasn't lived in it for years. I got a call from him today, and it sounded like something was wrong. He mentioned the house, so I came here to check on him." His mind flashed to the basement where Don had found T.J.'s lifeless body. His time at Turner House seemed so far away, and the cold and drafty mansion sitting in his periphery was now just an empty shell.

The officer turned Jamie's ID card over in his hands and examined it as if looking for something that would prove it fake.

"Do you have any idea where he is now?" the officer asked.

"None, but I've got to find him," he replied with desperation.

"All right. Well, your record's clean, so we're going to let you go. But if we see you back here, we won't be so nice next time. You can't just go breaking into houses that don't belong to you. We've got your number." The officer helped him out of the car, removed his handcuffs, and handed his driver's license back to him.

The two police cruisers blocking the Subaru pulled off to the side of the entrance so that Jamie could back out and pull away. He was just thankful that his story was good enough to work and that the police hadn't noticed the broken window in the back.

He looked up at the empty house and thought back to the last thing he'd typed on the Royal 1:

```
T.J.  had  another  opportunity  to
save those whose lives he'd affected
with the typewriter.
```

Maybe it worked better than I thought?

CHAPTER THIRTY-EIGHT

THE SUN PEEKED OUT OVER the horizon as Jamie made it back to Pittsburgh. After more than ten hours of driving between Pittsburgh and Cincinnati, he just wanted to rest his head a while although it was still swimming with thoughts of T.J. and the crash. *If the plan had worked, then why can I still remember everything? Is it because I typed the line?*

He slid his key into the door to the apartment as quietly as he could. Buttons growled on the other side of the door, and the dog let out a deep bark before Jamie could make it inside to comfort him. Lilly must have still been in bed.

As he knelt down to pet him, Jamie heard a voice from the other side of the couch.

"Where have you been?" Lilly asked in a cold tone.

He walked around to sit next to her. "I'm sorry. I had to go to Cincinnati." He decided to come clean because all of this was too much to keep from her any longer. "It had something to do with the wreck today."

Her scowl softened into a look of mournful sympathy. "So you know already?"

"Know what? What are you talking about?"

"You just took off after we got back. I tried to call you, but you wouldn't answer. That wreck yesterday. Your uncle died in it," she said, looking down at her lap.

The words knocked him backward. "Died? What do you mean? I went to see him in Cincinnati. I'm not sure how to even begin to explain it, but—"

"Cincinnati?" Lilly said. "Jamie, your uncle died on the bridge yesterday. Your aunt called me last night after you took off. She couldn't get a hold of you." She started to tear up.

"My aunt?"

"We have to go back up there. I took the next few days off. Deshawn said he'd keep an eye on the dog for us, and I already slid a copy of our key under his door."

Jamie said nothing. He had no idea what was going on.

"The way that you acted yesterday, it's like you knew. How did you know it was T.J. on the bridge?"

"I didn't," Jamie replied.

CHAPTER
THIRTY-NINE

THE HOUSE WAS NOTHING SPECIAL, just another modest prefabricated one-floor in the middle of a cookie-cutter subdivision. Lilly pulled the car into the driveway, and they walked the path to the front door. Jamie was still unsure of what was happening, but the empty house in Cincinnati and Lilly's odd mention of an aunt gave him a clue. His lack of sleep had made his mind fuzzy.

A woman was waiting for them behind the screen door. As soon as they got close enough, she pushed it open and ran to hug them.

"I'm so glad you're here," she said, throwing her arms around them and letting out a sob.

"I'm so sorry, Theresa," Lilly said. "I can't imagine what you're going through."

"I just can't believe he's gone," she replied.

The bland color of the walls brought Jamie back to their apartment in Pittsburgh. The place was modestly decorated, and the shelves were stacked with books.

They walked through the hallway to the kitchen, and Jamie stopped to look at a picture frame on the wall. It held several photos that reminded him of those that had fallen from T.J.'s journal, with one major difference. Jamie was looking at his college commencement. His dad stood to one side of him, arm wrapped around his shoulder, and T.J. stood on the other. The photo next to it was of T.J. holding him as a baby. Several other photos sat in the frame, all of Jamie and his uncle.

He stepped back into the living room. A framed wedding photo sat next to the armchair, showing Theresa and T.J. at the altar. Although the room was devoid of any macabre collectibles, it was sprinkled with the artifacts of a well-lived life.

Lilly sat at the kitchen with Theresa, who looked up at Jamie as he walked into the room. "He made the paper today," she said as he sat next to her. She slid the newspaper over to him.

Local Man Dies in Explosion after Saving Vacationing Family

Local steel mill worker, Thomas Joseph Lawson, perished in an explosion on Nathaniel Hale Bridge yesterday afternoon, but not before escorting three to safety. The explosion resulted from an overturned tanker truck; however,

the driver of the truck also escaped
unharmed.

"He went for a walk on the bridge and must have seen the accident," Theresa said. "The police told me that he had gone in and helped the family, but there was an explosion when he went back in for the driver, who'd apparently already made it out."

Jamie stared at the picture of the blaze. He must have gotten to the bridge a short time after the explosion and had missed T.J. by mere minutes.

They sat at the table and talked for quite a while. Jamie had to pretend that he already knew most of the things that Theresa said, but it was all completely new to him. This was not the same man who had locked himself away in a lonely mansion on a hill. T.J. had chosen a completely different life for himself, and evidence of that was reflected in the objects lining the walls and shelves of his home.

As they stood to leave, Theresa touched Jamie on the arm. "Your uncle left something for you. Hold on just a minute."

She disappeared around the corner, returned with a yellow file envelope, and handed it to him. On it, his name was written in T.J.'s handwriting.

"I didn't open it," she said, "but I think it's the book that he's been working on. He'd been toiling away in his office for the last few weeks. I found the envelope when I was going through his drawers to look for a copy of his will."

The three hugged and said their goodbyes.

"We'll see you at the funeral on Monday," Lilly said, opening the door to her car. "Let us know if you need anything in the meantime, and Mom's right up the road, so don't hesitate to give her a call."

Theresa waved to them as they pulled away.

"It's so sad. I can't believe that he's gone," Lilly said. "What did he leave you?"

Jamie dumped the contents of the envelope onto his lap. He picked up the thick stack of papers, loosely bound with packaging twine, and turned it over in his hands. It looked like an unpublished manuscript.

"Well?" Lilly asked impatiently.

"She was right. It's a manuscript."

Lilly pulled off at a gas station to fill the car. Jamie flipped through the pages of the manuscript, but it was a story with which he was already familiar. It was his own. As he started to tuck the pages back into the envelope, he noticed a smaller one inside. He slid it out and ripped open the seal. The paper was slightly yellowed, as if the note had been written a long time before. He recognized T.J.'s wiry handwriting and signature.

```
J,


Thanks for showing me the way. I
think that I've finally figured it
out! Never did go to Colorado, and
life has been a lot better for it.
```

Emily's all grown up now, and you should look up Louise sometime. I knew that you'd given me another chance to save them, but I had no idea that I would have a chance to save myself as well. Thanks for everything. And if all of this is gibberish, pay this letter no mind. Hope you enjoy the book.

T.J.

The pieces were starting to come together. Just as Jamie had relived this day, T.J. had been able to go back to the beginning. Instead of buying the house in Cincinnati, he must have moved to Pittsburgh to be close to the bridge. Without the typewriter to change their lives, his characters were saved, but this left T.J. with no way to prevent the crash that would kill Lilly. The flat tires were an insurance policy that she'd be nowhere near the bridge when the crash occurred.

Jamie scanned the note for several minutes. As the feeling of resolution set in, he realized he'd been holding his breath for some time and exhaled deeply. The muscles in his chest relaxed, and he sank into the car seat.

CHAPTER FORTY

S ARAH LAY FLAT ON THE massage table. The masseur was a thin muscular Italian man who was also shirtless for some reason. He worked his hands up and down Sarah's back. As he worked up to her shoulders, he leaned in and kissed her ear. Actually, it was more of a lick. He was licking her ear, but his tongue was small and sandpaper-like.

Theo barely escaped with his life as Sarah swung wildly to get the cat off her back. She pulled the covers off herself and slunk out of bed and into her house slippers. She flipped through the news headlines on her phone at the kitchen table while the coffee pot sputtered to life. The doorbell broke her concentration.

A delivery man held a small brown package out for her. Sarah thanked him and closed the door behind her. After pouring herself a cup of coffee, she sat back down at the kitchen table to open the box. She cut the packaging tape with her car key and lifted the flaps. It appeared to be a book, or at least a draft of a book. The pages were loosely bound together, and Sarah accidentally tore the first page while unwrapping it. She turned the stack over to read the title page.

```
              Correction Tape

                    by

              T.J. Lawson
```

What is this? A note had been handwritten at the bottom of the cover page.

```
Sarah,
Debated on whether or not to send
this to you. Found this in my
uncle's house after his death. Do
with it what you will, but thought
that you should have the chance to
read it.

Hope all is well in Cincinnati.

Jamie Lawson
```

Sarah flipped through to the dedication page of the manuscript.

```
Grief is a powerful thing. It can
cause us to turn away from those
we love, even from love itself.
It can cause us to seek refuge in
```

the safety of objects. Objects are harmless and predictable. They can't die, won't leave us, and can be tucked away on a shelf when we don't need them. But without love and the resilience that can come from inevitable losses, we'll become just like an object on a shelf, coated with dust and slowly rotting into irrelevance.

This book is dedicated to the unwitting participants in an ill-conceived experiment.

ABOUT THE AUTHOR

Chris Cooper was born in Cincinnati, Ohio in 1988. He currently lives in Cincinnati with his partner and Australian cattle terrier. You can stay up to date with Chris' latest publications at dreadfulmedia.com, follow him on Twitter @ ChrisCooper, peruse his mediocre photography on Instagram @DreadfulWriter, or explore his obscure fountain pen obsession at abetterdesk.com.